KNIVES

KNIVES

And Other Stories

Wendy Robertson

CHIVERS

British Library Cataloguing in Publication Data available

This Large Print edition published by AudioGO Ltd, Bath,
2013.
Published by arrangement with the Author

U.K. Hardcover   ISBN 978 1 4713 2304 1
U.K. Softcover   ISBN 978 1 4713 2305 8

Printed and bound in Great Britain by
MPG Books Group Limited

Introduction

In looking over this collection of stories written I find myself surprised at how much on the edge they seem: on the edge of society but also on the edge of darkness.

Some might say I have been influenced by three years working in prison with people who are on the margins and are consummate experts on the darker side of human experience. It's not that simple. The better truth is that I was drawn to work in prison because my own lifetime experience of living on the margins, of knowing my own edgy shadows.

Dark as these stories may appear they reflect my view of the shining recoverability of the human spirit and the qualities of stoicism, wit, humour and irony that aid survival and can bring about recovery and growth.

Some of these stories have been published elsewhere in anthologies. Others have been commissioned by newspapers and a museum. One has, quite surreally, been transformed into a manga comic. Some stories have their first outing in this collection. All of them go together to celebrate the wonder of people who make a shining thing from a life that might at first seem unlivable.

Wendy Robertson
Bishop Auckland

Contents

1 Queenie and The Water Man

Queenie Pickering's hat was always cocked at a cheeky angle. She was very particular about her appearance and was extravagant with her perfume: her favourites were *Rive Gauche* and *J'Adore*, a gift from her niece, Janine who was a flight attendant. Janine kept her auntie supplied with perfume and with liquor for her glass-fronted cocktail cabinet with the let-down shelf. The interior light—such an innovation when Queenie bought it in the Sixties—did not work now, and the mirrors and glass shelves were rarely dusted. But it was her pride and joy.

The first time this very unfortunate thing happened Queenie committed herself voluntarily to hospital; she praised the nurses and psychiatrists for their close care, despite her stifled resentment at their calling her Queenie, and not Miss Pickering. Her father's cousin Ralph had been the first one to call her Queenie at the age of six, when she was made May Queen at the carnival in her village. It was Ralph's son who took her to the pictures before he was posted to North Africa to fight Germans. Her father looked down on Tom because his cousin Ralph was a miner and was part of the world he thought he had left behind when he became a professional man. But Tom had liked her, loved her name. *'Queenie by name, queen of my heart.'* He wrote that in his very last letter, sent before he was blown up in the sands of Africa.

As she got older only Janine and two or three old friends called her Queenie. Everyone else in her world called her Miss Pickering. Two generations of schoolchildren in her village had called her Miss Pickering. Even when two of them, (grown up now and equipped with mobile phones and Ford Escorts), came upon her one midnight walking through the woodland clad only in her petticoat and armour-like brassiere, muttering lines from the poet John Clare—even these two likely lads called her Miss Pickering.

It was these young men's kindness and distress which made Queenie, that first time, decide she must seek help at the hospital herself. In the hospital the doctor gave her some pills so that when she got back home she no longer saw the Water Man rising, dripping pondweed and silvery fish, fairies dancing at his shoulder. And she missed him, this Water Man who smelled of almonds and honey wine.

After a long while, at the end of a particularly drab day, she decided to leave the pills in their bottle 'just for a day or so'. Then she breathed out, walked around and waited for the sparkle to come back in her life: she waited for the Water Man to arrive again. She put on her hat at its cocky angle, splashed

2

herself with *J'Adore* and set forth down her garden path.

Putting one foot before the other she started to smile broadly. The colours were brighter and the noises were louder. People swept by her in warm wafts of light. The buses roared and took on the aspects of scarlet tigers. The cars became insects bright as jewels.

She exclaimed and laughed at all this beauty. People on the pavement gave her a wide berth. She began to walk further and further afield, to drink in all the beauty and allow the Great Ones access especially the Water Man, her favourite. She began to return to her little house later and later. Even then, she would be just about ready to get into bed and the beauty of the world outside would call her and she just had to get up and go out again, to bathe in its dark luminescence.

One night she was actually in bed when some lines from Browning popped into her head.

'Thou, Soul, explorest—
Though in a trembling rapture—space
Immeasurable! Shrubs, turned trees,
Trees that touch heaven, support its frieze
Studded with moon and sun and star.'

She chanted the words again and again, racing through her back door and out through a space in her wicket fence towards the woodland. *'Trees that touch Heaven ... Trees that touch Heaven'*. She put up both her arms to join the trees in their touching.

The same young men, Ali Smith and George Onyatt, returning from a late drink at The Green Tree, saw her figure before them, fluttering in a long nightdress, hands waving. 'There she goes again, Ali!' George Onyatt gave chase and soon caught up with her. 'Come on, Queenie,' he said, his voice reasonable. 'This is no way to go on. No way at all.' He grabbed her arm.

She lifted her other hand and whammed him with her fist. 'Miss Pickering to you George Onyatt! Miss Pickering to you and to your father as well.'

He caught her hand in his. 'Come on, Queenie,' he mocked. 'Queenie's good enough for an old loony like you.'

That was when she brought his hand to her mouth and bit it, sinking her teeth to the bone. Howling like a hurt dog, he let her go and slipped to the floor.

She stood still before him, then looked at Ali Smith who had caught up with them. 'My name is Miss Pickering,' she said. 'You know that, don't you Alister?'

'Yes, Miss Pickering,' he said, taking her hand. 'So it is.'

That time she was taken into the hospital under a section and they gave her the pills that took away for a second time her visions of the giant trees and stars and her Water Man. She was a meek, very good patient. She helped with the tea rounds, taught a young girl to read, and she stayed tucked up in her bed all night, every night.

Her niece Janine visited her in hospital with a grey suited solicitor in tow. That day Queenie signed over all her affairs into her niece's capable hands. The hospital held a case meeting for Queenie. She recognised the chairman Len Crawshaw, who had once been and average pupil in her Scholarship Class. It was obvious to all there that Queenie was a prime candidate for Care in the Community, now not only fashionable but compulsory. When they checked her situation they found that her little house with its cocktail cabinet had been sold by her niece, who had gone off to build a new life for herself and her boyfriend Roger, in the depths of Canada.

But still they found her sheltered housing with a very kind warden. Queenie—for everyone called her Queenie now—Queenie could live there and the nurse could call every week to see that she was taking her medication. Everything would be Hunky Dory. Wasn't that how Care in the Community worked?

Queenie walked out of the sheltered house at the end of the first week. She put on her hat—not so smart now—packed all her most precious things, including a nearly full bottle of *Rive Gauche*, into three carrier bags. Then she caught the long distance bus to the town where they would not find her. Best to lie low, she thought. Best to lie low. The gleaming Water Man would be there she was sure. He was everywhere, so he would be in the city as well as the country. And the sky in the city would be studded with moon and sun and stars. And the trees would stride the earth.

*   *   *

'There we are, Queenie!' The pale faced girl smiled brightly as she ladled soup into the mug clasped in the old woman's faintly grimy hands. 'Buns at the end of the table, look.'

'Thank you. Kind of you, dear.'

The voluntary helper, (a pale, kind girl who was doing this a month before she went off to help build a school in Africa), watched the old woman in three coats waddle away to her accustomed place at the end of the table. Old woman? Maybe. You never knew how old these people were.

The brisk woman who had showed the girl the ropes here had said, 'Guess how old they look, dear, then take off twenty years.' That should make this old bird no more than sixty-five. Shame. The girl smiled brightly at the next customer, a young man who by that same formula must be no more than ten.

Queenie relished the soup and the thick bread. She had to dip the bread in the soup these days, as she was having trouble with two of her teeth on the right side. Terrible pains, she had. So much so today that there were thick knuckles of bread which she couldn't tackle, hungry as she was.

'Not want those, missis?' The young man who had followed her in the queue was sitting opposite her, slurping his soup. He nodded towards her rejected bread.

'No. No. Can't manage it dear. Teeth, you know!'

'Givin' you gyp, are they?'

Queenie pushed the hard lumps towards him and let her gaze wander away over his shoulder. She had to keep an eye on her bags, stacked carefully in the corner. She'd had her bags stolen once by some scallywag and that caused her real heartache. She lost the last of her perfume. That time in the face of her savage distress they had made her go into a supervised shelter for a week. Of course they reached for the pill bottle again, and those hypodermics. So she had run off from there, after taking a couple of their own Sainsbury carriers, stuffing them with a few things that were lying around. You never know when they'd come in useful. A brush. A bottle of ink. Some pillowcases. Two old cardigans. Some climbing socks.

Now she looked longingly into the bottom

of her cup.

'More soup?' The kind girl was beside her, a white enamel jug in her hand, like a Greek maiden on a vase.

Queenie nodded and held up her cup like a child.

'And was there something wrong with the bread?' The girl looked suspiciously at the man who was chewing away at the tough crusts.

'She give it to us,' he said defensively. 'She give it to us cause her teeth are giving her gyp.'

Queenie nodded. 'Back right, dear,' she said briefly. 'Don't know how it's happened. Always had perfect teeth. My father had his own teeth till he died, you know. Eighty-nine. Born when Victoria was on the throne.' She slurped the soup. 'But then, he knew teeth.'

'Did he?' said the girl. 'He knew teeth?'

Queenie nodded. 'Dentist,' she said.

'A dentist?' The girl's glance became brighter. 'There's a dentist here, Queenie. Calls here on Thursdays. He'll have a look at them. At your teeth. Stop them hurting.'

Queenie placed her cup on the stained bench and shook her head. 'No thank you dear. They'll take me inside. Lock me up again, like they did when I lost my bags. Pumping you full of rubbish.'

'Liquid coshes. That's what they use', said the young man. 'Use them in jail too. Ask anybody. Any more soup for me?' He put his mug under the girl's nose.

'Yes, good name that.' said Queenie. *'Liquid cosh.* Dulls you down so you can't live any more, or see things.' She paused. 'Things you want to see, that is.'

'No! No, Queenie,' said the girl eagerly, 'It's not like that. They don't want you to ...'

Queenie tied her third scarf round her neck, and her second scarf round her old hat. She fixed the girl with a look that had frozen many a child in Junior Three. 'Well, dear, you weren't there, were you?'

'Look!' said the girl desperately, 'They just take a look at you here, in that room back there. Then they can give you something to take the pain away. If you need any more than that, they can take you off to the surgery there and then, or make an appointment...'

'Surgery,' said Queenie, shaking her head.

'Whisky,' said the man. 'That's the best thing for toothache. They should give you whisky.'

The girl looked from one derelict to the other. It was not that you wanted gratitude. Sometimes all you wanted them to do was listen to you. She turned away, then turned back. 'Thursdays. This man comes on Thursdays, Queenie, between ten and eleven.'

'Whisky,' said the man. 'That's best.'

Queenie stood up and poked around inside her bags, checking the items to make sure nobody had stolen them while she was talking to that pushy girl. They taught them nothing nowadays. No restraint. No manners. She was pleased she'd had no children. Nothing but trouble. Children.

*   *   *

When Thursday came round Queenie had quite forgotten the conversation with the girl. She was surprised when, on that day, the girl brought a young man in an anorak and trainers to her end of the table.

'Queenie,' she said brightly. 'This is Jimmy O'Brien. He's a dentist and he could help you with that aching tooth of yours.'

'Dentist?' Queenie surveyed him from head to toe. 'He's not a dentist.'

The young man smiled a perfect-toothed smile. 'Now, what makes you say that, Queenie?'

'Well, first, you're dressed like a plough man, and second if you were a dentist you would call me by my right name. You'd have better manners.'

He slid onto the bench beside her. 'So what *is* your name?' She could smell a sickly smell of violets, mixed with lemon. Men smelling like women! A queer state of things. She moved to the very edge of the bench. 'Miss Pickering,' she said. 'That's my name.'

'Miss Pickering? Well, Miss Pickering,' he surveyed his smooth fingers, his perfectly

10

manicured nails. 'All I'm asking is that we go over into that little room there and you let me take a look at your mouth. Is it hurting now?'

'Yes,' she said reluctantly. 'Like that chap over there said. It's giving me gyp. Especially at night. With the cold.'

The dentist and the girl exchanged glances. Nights under bridges or in shop doorways would make teeth ache all right.

The girl coughed. 'Queenie ... Miss Pickering, she was telling me her father was a dentist, Jimmy.'

'Is that so? Well, Miss Pickering, he'd have told you that they shouldn't be neglected. Teeth.'

Queenie stirred. 'Well. No harm in letting you take a look-see, I suppose.' *Take a look-see.* She hadn't heard that for years. She had never even said it herself. That was how her father used to jolly up his patients.

The other two exchanged glances.

'I wouldn't have gone to him,' Queenie announced suddenly.

'Who?'

'My father.'

'Why not?' The young dentist was interested.

'He was never happier than taking the whole lot out and planting in a false set. He had a tidy mind, do you see? But it wasn't fair. Not fair at all. Some good teeth went in his bin. Some very fine teeth. My mother's teeth.

11

They went in his bin too. She never forgave him! He made her into an old woman in a morning.'

A frown marred the boy's brow. 'They did do that at one time. It would never be allowed now.'

'Well, consider him. Died in his eighties with a mouthful of teeth. Only three extractions. Not fair.' She paused. 'Mrs *Do As You Would Be Done By*!' she said suddenly.

'What?' Now he was entirely lost.

'A character in *The Water Babies*. Charles Dickens. The children in my class loved it. Mrs *Do As You Would Be Done By*. If he pulled out all their teeth he should have had that done to him. D'you see?'

'Well, Miss Pickering. As I say, we never take them all out now. We move heaven and earth to keep what's there, right in your mouth. I promise.'

Queenie got up, and reached for her bags. 'Very well. You can take a look.' And then, she fixed him with a severe glance. 'We'll see.'

In the little room was a dentist's chair of the more portable kind. The boy pulled on his rubber gloves and fixed a disposable bib over Miss Pickering's scarves. He talked to her all the time, concerned that if he left a gap in the talk, she would fly away from under his hand. He took a look at her mouth, this way, that way. His hands were gentle. Then he stood back. 'Look, Miss Pickering, would you like to get this over with now?'

'Over?' She was having problems, from her prone position, keeping her eye on her bags, which the girl had put in the corner.

'There are two in here which look a bit of a … look a bit poorly and need extracting. And one other which we might manage to save… If you come with me now…'

'Come with you?' She sat up straight. Her bags were still safe. 'Come with you? You might be Jack the Ripper. They said he was really a dentist.' She bustled past the girl and retrieved her bags. 'Or was it a doctor?'

'Janette here will come with us. You know Janette, don't you?'

'She has to give out the soup. She has a job.'

'They've let her off. So she can help you.'

Queenie pulled her hat down. 'Very kind of them I'm sure.'

'Will you come?' For the first time there was an edge to his voice. 'Will you come, for your own sake?'

She shrugged. 'Well, dear, if it means so much to you.'

*   *   *

Her face felt odd after he had taken the teeth out, as though only her eyes and her nose belonged to her and beneath them was a great yawning gap. And she was slavering! She only realised that when the slaver dropped

13

on to her coat. She couldn't even feel herself slavering. What were things coming to? One by one she smoothed out her scarves and tied them round her neck in the special way she had. The girl tried to help; tried to place her hat on her head. Queenie shook off the girl's hand. 'I can manage dear.'

It was all very strange but it was good to be without the pain.

'Now what shall we do with you?' said the girl called Janette, a bright, satisfied smile on her face.

'What shall you do with me? You? With me?' But the furious words which came out of her mouth were mumbled. She herself could not even understand what she said.

Janette and the dentist exchanged glances.

'Now, Miss Pickering,' said the boy dentist, taking off his rubber gloves. 'You need to be very careful, just for a little time. A day, two at the most. Just so no cold gets into that jaw. Just till that local wears off. So we have a bed in the ward here...'

She mumbled again. 'No. No bed.'

'I know you don't like it, but I promise, promise you that you'll be out in a day, two at the most.' The girl looked quite desperate.

Promises. Piecrusts. She looked at the earnest young face above her. The child meant it. Meant it of course. She did mean to be kind. But she didn't realise. She didn't know what they did with you, once they got you in there.

14

They took your bags away and put them in the incinerator. They inveigled you into a bath. They couldn't wait to wash the smells of the street out of your hair. Then they got out their rattling bottles.

Still, Queenie meekly allowed Janette to settle her comfortably in the waiting room while she went off to sign some forms or other for the dentist. Then Queenie stood up and crept, with only the barest rustle of her bags, out of the room, out of the building; she was down one of her favourite and familiar back streets before the ink was dry on the dentist's form.

There was this little park, a mere strip of green, where the Water Man would be waiting. He was always there at one forty five. Every day. Never missed. They had a long term arrangement. He'd be there, smelling of almonds and honey wine.

2 Chaos

The screaming of brakes. The noise of traffic in my ear. Lions roaring like people. People growling like lions. It was that noise of the traffic that struck me the time I met Anne Marie.

And it's noise that gets me, even now.

It splits off in shards. The shards splinter into points of light. It crashes on rock surfaces and shatters again. Crashing, then breaking again. Noise and light.

I was reading about Chaos Theory on one of those cards. You know? You get them on the back of packets of herb tea in a series called Educational Resolutions.

I get to read a lot now. Like it. It started when I was inside prison. Twenty hours locked away and you certainly have time to read. *True Romance. True Crime. Serial Killers On The Rampage.* All that sort of thing. Dark. The books huddle close together on the library shelves. I tell you some of those books smell of rotting meat and looked as though someone had been chewing them. I suppose there's not a lot to do behind the door. There are few ways to give yourself a bit of comfort: contemplating darker lives than your own is one of them.

I read other books in there too. I read

Sigmund Freud in there. He met some very funny women didn't he? But, you will say, no funnier than me. And I really took to this guy Carl Gustav Jung interpreting dreams and all that. Of the two of them I have to say I prefer Carl Gustav. Dreams. Dreams. You do a lot of dreaming on twenty hour lockdown. Carl Gustav makes a lot of sense to me.

Even now, on the out, I still read a lot. But I save my reading for when Jake's out, or in bed. Jake's my husband—he was John when I met him. That was before he went on a course called *How To Re-invent Yourself.* Anyway, like I say, I save my reading for when he's at work. Not that he'd disapprove... well, not of me *reading*, that is. He'd say it's about time I made an effort. But I don't tell him about it because then he'd kind of own it.

And that's the last thing I want.

For years John—er, Jake—used to let me know just how thick he thought I was. Well, he wouldn't exactly use the word *thick*. When we were first married, before even we had Janine, he did this course on *Anger Management.* 'Do you realise, Lilah, that Words can be Blows? That it is *a violence* to Withhold Affection?'

So I had to roll back over and let him do it again. I was not allowed to withhold myself because it was *a violence*.

Violent? I was never violent. My mother, rest her soul, she was very violent. But then she was mad. My father was violent too, but

17

that was because he was real bad. But me? Mild as mother's bloody milk, I am. Wouldn't say Boo! to a rattlesnake.

Jake made excuses for me. He would say to our dinner guests. 'Lilah here lost so much school with TB when she was a nipper, you know. No provision, then. No wonder she never caught up, poor soul.'

Jake and I actually had dinner parties in those days. He took a lot of trouble over the dinner parties; set the table the night before, instructed me line-by-line about the food. We lived at the end of this cul-de-sac in a warren of cul-de-sacs on the biggest bloody chi-chi housing estate in England. Ticky boxes.! And to think that estate sits cheek by jowl with the prison where I was eventually to get my much delayed education.

(Dinner parties! My mother would have laughed her head off about those dinner parties. She's dead now of course and can only laugh in my dreams. I saw her once at the top of the stairs. She was all in yellow, her eyes, her arms wide open in greeting. That was after she died, of course.)

Anyway when I got out of jail I had to keep all my reading a secret. Like I say I couldn't do with Jake busily, busily making me less *thick*. Some of the books he pushed onto me started out with our Janine, of course. She's very clever, my Janine. Top of her nursery, top of her class, top of her college. These days she

18

earns the biggest bonuses in her section of her merchant bank.

(I had this other dream where I tell my mother that her granddaughter is a merchant banker dealing in *futures*. 'Futures?' she shrieks in that cackling voice of hers. 'Futures? Well, you tell her that's what comes from having a gypsy for a grandma.' I woke up laughing but dared not tell Jake. He loathed my mother almost more than he loathed Anthony Wedgwood Benn).

And Janine plays the piano. Can you believe it? She sings too. Low and throaty like Sarah Vaughan. She was A Daddy's Girl, of course, from start to finish. As soon as I conceived her Jake read this book called *How To Raise A Genius*. He used to play tapes to her, chant rhymes into her ear from the day she was born; 'training her up to greatness', he called it.

You can tell, can't you that Janine was *his* from the start: his personal experiment? He chose her games for her, her friends, her books. He chose her O Levels and A levels. He sat alongside her and read all her set books with every course. He careered round the country with her to sort out just the right university. Five offers! She had her pick. He took all her successes very personally as though they were his, not hers.

And of course, he drove her to college on that first day: our old Renault piled with luggage, heaped with books, plants, kettles. He was almost drooling with delight. It was their own special adventure. *Two Go To College. Jan and Jake Abroad.*

She said to me, 'Won't you come, Mum? You'll be company for dad, all the way home.'

I was flattered. 'Would you like me to come, Janny?'

Jake exploded. 'No need, no need. We all know your mother has other things to do, Janny. In any case you know your mother cries at the drop of a hat. You wouldn't want her to embarrass you, would you?' Then he laughed that neighing laugh of his, yanked the door open, swept off his baseball cap and ushered her into the car.

So I keep my reading these days a secret, hide the books in the back roof space with the bottles and the cigarettes.

Where was I?

Chaos Theory.

Chaos Theory says everything is connected, even the most random and chaotic events. What a great idea! When I read it on the herb tea card I hugged it to me. Then I found this book of photographs on the market: computer simulations of Chaos Theory. Like works of art. See? The camera pulls back and back, see? And what seems to be random specks become swirls, and the swirls become a great design.

Almost makes you believe in God, doesn't it? I couldn't say that to Jake, of course. He's through his Buddhist phase now and into

Humanism. Cardboard coffins, poems over the grave and guitars and all that.

Talk about *chaos*.

*   *   *

So now we get back to this screaming of brakes. This noise of traffic in my ear. The lions roaring like people. The people growling like lions. And this girl. Her hand was digging in my shoulder. I could hardly see her through the haze, but I knew from the very scent of her she was young. What was she saying?

I opened my eyes so wide my eyelids hurt. The stud in the girl's tongue glittered like the morning star; her tongue was red, red as a garden poppy. Her teeth were sharp and gleaming,

She gripped me tight. 'Hey you! Whatcha thinkyer doin'?' Her voice was warm, rough as a puppy's bark. 'Just about bought it then, din'cha?'

'Let go! Let go of me, will you?' I found my voice at last and shouted against the roar of the traffic.

She loosened her grip and I fell back against a wall. 'An'-thank-you-very-much...' Now she was a sulky puppy chanting the words. 'Thank-you-very-much-Anne-Marie-for-saving-me-from-frigging-certain-death.'

Her hand, when I grabbed at it, was remarkably soft. My lips would not stretch properly round the words. 'Sorry... I'm sorry. How d'I get here? One minute the bottom of Pilgrim Street. Then next out here. Cars. Lions. Lorries. Oh dear!' I had to turn quickly to one side so the spewing vomit didn't catch her. My throat burned and my mouth felt filthy.

Then she laughed. Her smile dimmed the glitter of the afternoon sun. 'Lions! Whoops! Been on the pop have we? Here, get hold of my arm. There's bogs at the station. Nice wash and brush up and we won't know the difference.'

The toilets were empty. The girl removed my bulky shoulder bag, peeled me out of my coat, ran a basin of water for me and watched while I splashed my face and hair. I rubbed my hands on the stringy roller towel.

She held out my coat. 'There what did I tell yah? Better, innit? Getcha coat back on. I'll button you up. Here's your bag. Now no one'll know the difference.' She hung my bag on my shoulder.

My vision cleared and I took a closer look at her. 'I've seen you before. I know you.' She was probably one of Jake's ex-pupils. All sorts they are. All sorts.

'And I seen you! That purple coat with the big buttons and the swagger back. Couldn't miss it. At the station every Friday on the button. That friggin' purple coat.' Her tone told me just how naff my coat was. 'Yeah. I

seen you. Give me many a ten pence ancha?'
She assumed what was obviously an alien
voice. *'Can yer spare us ten pence for a cup
o' tea missis?* Give us ten pence every time,
dincha? But only on the way back to the train
when...'

I pulled on my gloves. 'When I'm the worse
for wear?'

'You said it, darlin', not me.'

I loved this girl now. I loved her hair. I
loved the lemon scent of her. I loved her smile
with its glittering stud. I loved her like she was
my own daughter. 'Here, Anne Marie—was
that your name?—Why can't I take you for a
cup of tea? We can have a cup of tea together.'

She eyed me narrowly. 'Yah're not a dyke,
are yeh?'

I knew the word from the television. 'Nah.
Don't be silly.'

'Anyway, I'm wasting time standing here.
Could've made a fiver, the time it's taken to
clean you up.'

I was desperate now. I wanted her to stay. I
didn't want to lose her. 'Look, come for a cup
of tea in the buffet here ... and I'll give you a
fiver. I'm still a bit shaky, you know?'

'We-ell, put like that. But not friggin'
coffee. Lager's better. Caffeine's bad for you.'

See what I mean about chaos?

*   *   *

Her name was Anne Marie and she had dense black spiky hair and black lines around her eyes. They were bright, those eyes: birdlike and cold.

We didn't say much to each other in the café. She didn't tell me her life story and I didn't tell her mine. She coughed quite a bit. We peered into our drinks and talked about the weather.

'What you think about this friggin' rain?' she said. 'It's rained every day for a week. Wreaks havoc with the graftin'. Friggin' rain.'

'It must be hard on you, out in all weathers...'

Christ! I sound like one of those long nosed women Jake got to come to the dinner parties. 'Do you have a flat or something?'

'Flat? You jokin' aren't you?'

'So you sleep outside, like?'

'So we do. Until the friggin' filth moves us round. It's their pastime, moving us around in the early hours.'

'How do you manage to sleep?'

'Mostly I don't sleep. I stay awake.'

'Stay awake? How do you manage that?

'Well, If I've had a good day I stay awake with a little help from my old friend Whizz.'

'Whizz? Is that your boyfriend?'

*　　　*　　　*

She was still laughing when she helped me to

24

buy my ticket and put me on the train. It was only when I got home that I found my purse had been lifted.

The next day I went back to the road by the station, sober this time, to find the girl called Anne Marie coughing her guts out on the pavement. I didn't ask her about the purse, just bundled her back onto the train and brought her home. Here. Where I live.

*   *   *

Of course Jake didn't like it when I brought Anne Marie home. I heaved her into the sitting room, closed the door, then turned to face him.

'You want her to stay *here*, Lilah? The girl smells. It's a big mistake. I won't have it.' His face was yellow as wrinkled custard.

Anne Marie didn't smell of anything except lemons. Jake always accused people he didn't like of smelling. 'She'll die out there, Jake. Out in the street. She has pneumonia. Listen to that cough.'

His yellow face was turning to purple, like a bruise. His hands kept curling into fists, then going loose. I wondered if he was remembering those *Anger Control* seminars. How I wished he would hit me. At least that would be a touch.

It was twenty odd years since he had touched me. It's like he made a hobby of avoiding it: avoiding touching me. I don't know what started that off. Probably Janine. Once he had Janine's hand to hold, once he had her to tickle and to cuddle, he didn't need anyone else. Oh no! I'm not suggesting anything funny, like the stuff I heard about in prison. Not at all. A daughter was all Jake needed. Not a wife.

Now I watched him carefully. 'She can go in Janine's room.'

I could hear his teeth grinding. Then, 'No, I tell you. What has got into you, you stupid woman? There are hospitals. She should go to the hospital.'

'She won't go to hospitals. There's Janine's room, isn't there? She never comes home now.'

'No! I'm telling you no.'

'Just a week or so, Jake, until she feels better.' I keep my voice mild, entirely lacking in defiance. It sometimes works.

'No!' he shouted. 'No!' He took a step towards me, his fist curled tight now. The sitting room door opened and there was Anne Marie hanging off the doorjamb. 'Well!' she gasped, 'You didn't tell us your husband was a wanker, Lilah.'

He turned from me to her, then back again. He spluttered 'Oh! Oh!' Then he grabbed his anorak off its specified peg and slammed out of the house.

Anne Marie croaked out a laugh, then

slithered down the doorjamb in a half faint.

'Now, pet,' I said, getting one arm under her arm and round her shoulders. 'Let's get you into bed.'

*   *   *

So there you have it. Jake took that one look at Anne Marie and stayed away. He retired to the little box room he will insist on calling his study. He was permanently yellowish-white with anger. I hadn't seen him look so shaken since the billy-goat cornered him on the farm where we spent our honeymoon: the highlight of a very dreary holiday for me. We never went back to the country after that. Jake took to pontificating that the country was very much overrated as a holiday destination.

After the honeymoon our holidays consisted of Paris alternating with Bruges, year in year out. Paris bleeding Paris. Bruges boring Bruges. You wouldn't think you'd be bored with Paris would you? I can't tell you I how pleased I was when the Berlin Wall came tumbling down and Jake raised his sights. The riverboats in Budapest and Prague were a bloody marvellous change from those fucking *bateaux mouches.*

Where was I? Oh yes. Jake avoided Anne Marie as though she were a resident tarantula. That very first morning he crept out to work at seven o'clock. Scared stiff of seeing her over

27

the cornflakes. See?

He needn't have worried. It took me three days to get her temperature down and her head off the pillow. You'll be impressed when I say I didn't have a single drink in that time. Motivation, sec? I was wary that Jake would come home at an odd hour and throw her out. But luckily he was well into his usual routine of staying after school for meetings, followed by tea in the domestic science department with Miss Flagg, who is a Fellow Humanist. Then on Tuesdays he would go on to his Steam Train Society with his friend Roland who's an accountant. Wednesdays he went to Nineteenth Century Literature. Thursdays it was his class in Mandarin Chinese.

It was when Anne Marie got up and started moving round the house properly on Saturday that Jake snapped. Late on the Saturday night I was lying in bed when I heard the telephone downstairs tinkle. I picked up the bedroom phone and ear-wigged the call. Jake was ringing Janine.

'Dad? I haven't got much time. I'm researching South American Metals for this meeting tomorrow...'

'It's your mother, Janny, she's...'

'Dad? Is she ill, is she...?'

I have to say it is quite nice to hear the thread of worry in my daughter's voice.

'What is it, Dad?' she says urgently.

'Ill? No. Worse than that…'

'Dad!'

'There is a creature…'

'Creature?'

'She brought this creature into the house. I'm afraid your mother has lost it, Janine. We both know she's always been, well, ten pence to the pound. Look at your grandmother. Mad as a hatter. But this! This is crazy, Janny.'

'What is this creature Dad? A gerbil? A cat?'

'It's a girl. A street girl?'

'A prostitute?'

'She's probably that as well, I shouldn't wonder. She lives on the street. She has cut marks on her arms and she has—dare I say it—the odour of the street about her.'

There's a rustling at Janine's end. A man's voice, surly and tired, calls, 'Jaye! It's cold! Come to bed!' Then both Jake and I can hear a door click shut.

Jake coughs.

Janine says, 'Now, Daddy, what do you mean she's brought a street girl in?'

'Found the creature begging at Newcastle station. Of course I warned her. But she has taken this folly into her head. It's just too bad. I came home today to find stinking trainers in the hall and…'

'Do you mean she's staying there? The creature?'

'Janine.' He pauses. 'She's put the creature

in your bedroom...'

Bored, bored with his voice and with hers I crash down the receiver and hope they notice.

* * *

On the following Monday, with Jake safely at work, Anne Marie came downstairs looking surprisingly perky. Her hair was drawn back in one of Janine's scrunchies and she was wearing a neat tee-shirt and jeans. Jake insisted that we always keep these in Janine's bottom drawer in case she returns home unexpectedly. I'm not quite sure why we do this. Would she come home naked, do you think? She would hardly leave her designer stuff behind, would she?

Anyway, apart from the dense blackness of her hair Anne Marie might have been anyone's daughter in this ticky-tacky street. *They're all made of ticky-tacky and they all look just the same.* That's the song isn't it?

Anne Marie threw my purse on the kitchen table. 'You didn't go through my bag?' she said. 'You would have found your purse.'

'It's your bag, pet,' I said. 'I wouldn't go in your bag,'

Plastic shrieked on plastic as she pushed it across the shiny Laura Ashley table cover. 'I'd have thought you'd be keen to get it.'

I left it where it was. 'Why d'you take it?' I said.

She shrugged. 'Because it was there. Force

of habit. Begging. Robbing. It's a way of life.'

I waited for her to tell me something about herself, but she didn't. She never did tell me too much about herself. Suddenly she leaned forward over the table and I could see the darker skin under her eyes and the fine down on her cheek. 'Why d'you get together with him? That Jake? He's an ugly bugger, and that friggin' voice! Like a strangled cat.' She blinked. 'And you! Well you're not bad looking, even now.'

'Bloody good of you,' I said.

'Don't mention it.' Her lips turned up into a childlike, self-satisfied grin, and her smile ignites mine.

'Why?' she persisted. 'Different as chalk and cheese, you two. Even talk different. You talk, well, let's say *common*, compared with him. How d'you meet him?'

I stared at her. 'Well, he was an ugly bugger then, Anne Marie, and entirely without charm. No one in their right mind would have had him. But then me, I was the daughter of a mad gypsy who didn't know her arse from her elbow. The two of us had been thrown out of our house. He had a house. He had a job and I didn't. And he was clever. Always spouting stuff. Seemed harmless enough then. But...'

'But in the house he thinks he's bloody Hitler,' she nodded. 'I've heard him.'

'You've been listening!'

She shrugged. 'Friggin' thin walls, these

31

houses. Tacky.' She looked round. 'Any lager in this *ken*?'

'Just beer.' I hauled some of Jake's bottles of real ale from the pantry, opened a bottle of red wine and placed them on the table. We drank through the morning in quiet companionship. There was talk. She painted a picture for me: of life in care as some kind of bloody apprenticeship in the arts of fending off unwanted advances, of robbing and the use of substances. I told her about my mother who was the daughter of a true Romany and went mad in the end with the confinement of a house. Especially because it was Jake's house. How even in her more rational times my mother would howl to the full moon, wailing that living *in brick* was no fate for a true Romany.

'*In brick*?' Anne Marie whistled appreciatively.

Then she leaned across the table and took hold of my hand. 'I tell yer what, Lilah, let's have a bit of fun. We'll go down to Newcastle and do a bit of grafting.'

*   *   *

Months later the expensive lawyer Janine had hired for me tried to make out it was the red wine that did it. That in my weakness I was led on by a wicked girl to steal all that jewellery: the stuff that was weighing down my pockets when I was arrested. My own lawyer blamed Ann Marie right there, in the court. I intervened there and then and told the judge that day was the best bloody time I'd had for twenty years. That I had enjoyed myself. And that Anne Marie, the girl in question, had none of the goods—none at all—on her. Had she? How did they know it was not *me* who was leading her astray? Wasn't I the grown-up?

Still, my counsel still tried to defend me against myself. So finally I had to shut him up by telling the judge to send the police to search the back loft of my house where they would find the perfume and the razors, the hairdryers and handbags that were my booty from all those years going up and down to Newcastle every Friday. I had been doing it for years. As I said to the judge, in many ways meeting Anne Marie was very nearly the saving of me.

But not quite.

Prison was bad but not too bad. Being older meant that some of the young girls made a bit of a mum of me. That was a protection in its own way. Jake visited the prison, but I told them I would not see him. For the first time in more than twenty five years I could live through twenty-four hours without the constant drip of Jake's presence around me. I relished this wonderful freedom.

Janine came to see me every month and at first I could have sworn that she seemed more interested in me, now in prison, than ever she had been. But I must have been mistaken, because just before my release she took up a very well paid job in Mexico City and neither Jake nor I have seen or heard from her since.

Anne Marie did try to visit me in jail once, but was turned away because she didn't have the proper pass. She told me so in one of her letters, the first one with an Israeli postmark. *Then afterwards, Lilah, I went back to your house and tried to talk to old buggerlugs Jake about you. Do you know what? He tried it on with me! His hand on my bare knee! I socked him where the sun don't shine and that stopped him in his tracks.*

I sat in my cell and had a great laugh at that. Then I got to thinking maybe I might have made some difference to Ann Marie. She's out there in the sunshine, after all. And not coughing. I told her time and again that she needed to get to the sun.

I read her letter many times. You do that in prison. Read your letters again and again. In time you can recite them like poems. As I re-read her letters I was struck by how very well she wrote. Fluent. Witty. There was a lot about Anne Marie that I never knew.

Best of all, there in prison, I could read what I wanted without it improving my female consciousness. I could plunder the library shelves on my own. That was how I found Freud and Jung, Lord Byron and William

Blake. And Dean Koonz and Stephen King. There was even this book on the origins of trading in tea in the British Empire. That was a very old book.

Of course when I got out Jake was still here in my ticky-tacky house, waiting. These days he looks thinner and uglier than ever and has nothing to say to me. He is probably missing Janine, who is out there in Mexico with her new husband. He keeps her postcards under his pillow. As well as this, I think he might be that bit scared of me. I can't think why.

I sleep in Janine's room now and he doesn't challenge my desertion. He's stopped going to all his clubs and courses and comes straight home from school. Miss Flagg has rung three times but he won't come to the phone. He eats in front of the television and I eat in the kitchen. He is barely visible to me in our everyday life. Perhaps he fears that he will become so transparent as to render himself entirely invisible; that he will not only fade from my life but fade from the life of the world as well.

Sometimes, like I say, I hear these crashes and rushing noises. Sometimes I see spangles and stunning cartwheels of light. Sometimes the light becomes solid, breaks off in bright shards and crashes onto the hard kitchen floor. It gets tangled in the cobwebs that hang under the table and between the chairs; it settles on the tufts of grass growing between the tiles.

Cut glass. Spiky shards. Frost on grass.

It nearly drowns me at times, all this light and sound. But it is all right. From the moment I read those cards on the tea packets and saw the pictures in that book, it made sense.

Chaos.

The world has been in chaos since the day I was born. But now I know that chaos melts again into glorious scintillating form and I am safe. I would like to tell all this to Jake as he shuffles round the house but I can't. We don't talk at all now. I suppose that's just as well, when you think of it.

3 My Name is Christine

Christine Cazelet was taken into care at the age of eleven because her mother would not listen to her, and would not stop her cousin Seamus Bates coming to take care of her and her little sister Sallyanne on Saturday nights when their mother went clubbing and their father went to play snooker.

Christine kept her mouth shut for eighteen months, wary of Seamus' threat to kill her if she spoke about it, if she told on him. Of course, he said that would be after he'd killed Sallyanne before her eyes. He would take her little sister and make her bleed to death like a stuck pig. He said.

There was no telling her mother and father. She couldn't tell them how Seamus said that it always hurt at first, and every girl learned this terrible thing from someone who loved them, before they could grow up and go into the world.

At school Christine would look around and wonder who else was learning this savage lesson. Which other girl was enduring this, amongst her own Teddy Bears and her own Sindy Dolls, her own plasticine and paints?

Christine begged her mother not to go out on a Saturday night. She begged her not to leave her with Seamus. As she clicked down the street in her high heels, her mother would laugh with her friends, talking about how their Christine was getting so clingy these days. She was getting on Len's nerves. Mrs Cazelet had worked hard all week in the shop, and Saturday night was her reward. Dancing. That was such a great buzz. Len had his snooker, she had her dancing. It was only fair.

And she was so lucky with young Seamus. He even made the girls their supper. And young Sallyanne idolised him. Christine had idolised him too, until she started this thing about wanting her mother there all the time. Mrs Cazelet would pull off Christine's clinging hands and say, 'Stop it, will you? You're too old for this.'

That night Seamus called Christine a monster several times and told her that if she made a fuss with her mother on a Saturday night again he would kill Sallyanne and throw her body over the cliff into the North Sea. After that Christine stopped making any fuss at all. Her mother petted her, said what a good girl she was now, and brought her a new Sindy doll.

From then on Christine was quiet in the house and quiet at school. One day in the toilets she heard a girl telling another about a trip to the fair, with her father and her cousin, Declan.

'Your cousin Declan,' said Christine, coming up to stand too near the girl, 'Do you like him?'

The girl looked at her, hard. 'Yeah. He's all right. He's brilliant.'

'Does he … Does he…' Christine said desperately. 'Does he do things to you?'

The girl laughed. 'Do things? He ties me to a tree when we play cowboys.'

'Does he do other things?' Christine persisted. 'To you.'

The girl turned and pushed her so hard she fell against a basin. 'What're you talking about?' she shouted. Then she grabbed her friend. 'Come on, gerrout of here. That lass is mad. That Christine Cazelet is mad.'

Their steps rang hollowly on the tiles and the door clanged behind them. Christine looked at herself in the mirror and saw her own anxious face, wide-browed and large-nosed. She laid her hot brow against the cool glass. She brought it right back then lay it on the glass again. Then she butted the glass like a goat. Harder. Harder. On the fifth bang the glass splintered and her blood was running down the wall, down her face. The pain pierced her but the running blood seemed to let the worst of the feeling out of her body. She poked out a splinter of mirror and looked at it through the film of blood. Then she put her palm on the wall in front of her and scraped the splinter across the back of her hand, welcoming the cleansing pain which streaked through her again.

She could not go to the classroom now, because they would all see what she had done. She would just sit down and have a little rest and when the bleeding stopped and the pain stopped she would go home.

Twenty minutes into the lesson Miss Murray, her teacher, missed her and asked if anyone had seen Christine? Two of the girls exchanged glances. 'She was in the toilets Miss. We left her in the toilet. She was saying daft things.'

Later Miss Murray stayed with Christine in the ambulance and in the hospital. She met the mother there, hauled by a telephone call from the shop where she worked. 'What happened, what happened?' Mrs Cazelet said, taking Christine by her undamaged hand.

'There was an accident,' said Miss Murray. 'She fell against the mirror.'

'Fell? Fell?' Mrs Cazelet bent down bringing her face close to her daughter's. Christine's bland eyes surveyed her from beneath the head bandage. 'Did you fall or were you pushed? Who did this to you?' said Mrs Cazelet. 'I'll have them. Wait till I tell your Dad.'

Very slowly Christine shook her head. 'I can't tell. I'm not supposed to tell.'

A month later, when her wounds were nicely healed, Christine smashed the mirror again in the girl's toilets. This time she used her shoe on the very edge of the mirror. It

40

was only the edge, so she could get a single splinter. This time she cut her arm above the cardigan line. She felt the mantle of relief thrown over her as the blood started to trickle. Then she pulled down her cardigan sleeves and went back to the classroom.

Twenty minutes later Miss Murray, patrolling the rows, saw the sticky trail of blood leading away from the exercise book, in which Christine was writing. The trail led down the side of the desk into a pool on the floor.

This time Christine was bandaged up at a local surgery. Miss Murray rang the headmistress to say she thought they should contact a social worker. When she got back into the surgery Christine had gone. She followed her and spotted her making her way along the road away from the school. Miss Murray followed her, keeping her distance.

Christine ran the few hundred yards to the edge of the town and along the cliff edge. Miss Murray's footsteps speeded up, then slowed again as she saw Christine sit down at one of the seats that were placed on the cliffs for people to look out to sea.

The sea was its usual slate grey but there had been heavy winds and the breakers were smashing against the cliff, the spray leaping into the air and catching the light like silver fish.

Miss Murray plonked herself down beside the girl. She spread her long, trunk-like legs before her. She smelled of mint and old cigarettes. 'Well now, Christine. Why? Why do you do it?'

Christine glanced at her. 'I don't know, Miss.'

'Come on. You can't hurt yourself like that and not know why.'

'I don't know why, Miss.'

'Did you want a ride in the ambulance again?'

Christine shook her head.

'Did you want me to pay you some attention?'

The girl frowned up at her. 'I wanted to hide it from you, Miss.' She clasped her arm. 'Under my cardigan.'

There was a long silence, Miss Murray said, 'What did it feel like, when you did it?'

A vague smile crossed Christine's lips. 'Good. It felt OK.'

There were more conversations after that, with the headteacher, with social workers and a man in an office who tapped his own hand a lot with his pencil. Christine's mother was defensive but genuinely bewildered. It affected her so much that she couldn't face dancing on three Saturday nights, so she stayed in. In all that time Christine did not hurt herself again. Even so, she was as quiet as ever.

Then Mrs Cazelet decided she was due for a night out and called on her nephew Seamus. Christine heard the call and went up to the bathroom and looked at herself in the mirror. She remembered the clanging sirens of the ambulance bell and Miss Murray's anxious face. She opened the door to the bathroom cabinet and took out one of her father's yellow disposable razors, and put it in her cardigan pocket.

Then she went down, put on her padded jacket, thrust two bananas in the pocket alongside the razor and set out. She was four miles away when they found her trudging along the clifftop, the hood of her jacket pulled up against the driving rain. In her pocket was the rotting peel of a banana.

Still, they didn't find the razor in her pocket.

Mrs Cazelet admitted that Christine was quite beyond her control. 'You see this?' she said to the social worker. 'Look around you. A loving home. Everything she needs. What can I do?' She threw up her hands in genuine despair. 'For her own safety, for her own safety? Perhaps for a little time. A rest. Till she realises she mustn't run…'

Christine Cazelet was taken into care because she couldn't make her mother listen.

*   *   *

In the residential school Christine Cazelet came up against Phoebe Bliss, known to everyone as Tigger. Compared with Christine's tall bony bulk, Tigger was tiny: small face, small feet. Her fingers were very short, giving her hands the appearance of paws. She had a very wide mouth and a very foul vocabulary, which Christine soon learnt to share.

After one or two fist fights (which Christine finally let Tigger win) they became best friends. This involved dodging about together a bit, playing snooker with the boys and mostly beating them. It involved telling ghost stories in the dark. It involved sharing and exchanging clothes (although this was not always easy, because of the difference in their sizes). It also involved recognizing the truth of the fact that the rest of the world was their enemy.

The two girls regularly patrolled the ragged, neglected beauty of the extensive gardens attached to the house, which had once been the home of a wealthy shipbuilder. The very long, very high stone wall all round the grounds that had once kept poachers out now kept recalcitrant children in. In the garden Christine and Tigger climbed trees, smoked skinny spliffs and the stolen cigarettes.

They didn't speak with each other about just why they were there. In fact Christine didn't know, quite, why she was there. After her mother finally washed her hands of her, the social had placed her with a foster family in a big, sprawling house. There were two other foster children already in the house: more flotsam and jetsam beached up in the care system. These girls, Flora and Jenny, were so thrilled to be there, so busy playing mummies and daddies that Christine wanted to vomit.

The place was run by Jo, a kindly, solid, foster mum who knew her stuff. 'We only have two rules here, Chris ...' she said.

'Christine,' said Christine, her glance sliding round Jo to take in the brightly lit fish tank that was built into the wall. 'My name is Christine.'

'... only have two rules here, Christine.' said Jo. 'One is you must turn up for tea at six o'clock. The other is you always let me know where you are. That's why mobile phones were invented. Oh! And everyone does one job off the list every day.' She nodded at the extensive list stuck to the fridge. This list covered every household task from mopping the hall floor to cleaning the taps. 'Oh, and if you just tick them we'll know the job's done. No good doing a job twice, is there?' She beamed, showing her large, perfectly formed teeth which stuck out very slightly.

'That's three,' said Christine.

'What?' said Jo.

'Three rules.' Christine put her head down and wouldn't meet Jo's gaze.

In the management of her foster home, Jo had her own very powerful secret weapon, which appeared on the table every day at six o'clock. She was a stupendous cook. Perfect pies, perfect burgers, perfectly succulent chips, mashed potatoes soft as snow, chops tender as jelly. The array was endless. She was just as good at sweets: lemon meringue pie, trifle, fruit salad.

The other two kids, Flora and Jenny, glugged all this up and felt well and truly fostered. Christine ended up thinking that Jo just fostered children so she had a regular and appreciative audience for her cooking. Still, Christine herself glugged alongside the others. In the four months she survived at Jo's she put on nearly a stone in weight. Her face rounded, her limbs rounded and, most horrible of all, her breasts swelled.

She felt stranded on Mars, on Jupiter, the other side of the sun. Sometimes she saw all their mouths opening and closing and couldn't hear what they were saying. Jo's husband, Max, was quieter than Jo; his coming and going from his job at the council was an automatic part of the household, like the whirring of the washer and the tea on the table at six o'clock. One day he looked over his paper and winked in a comradely fashion at Christine and her heart went into spasm. She stopped eating her tea, fled upstairs and locked her door. Jo came up after half an hour and, after pleading to be let in, banged hard on the door. 'Let me in, Chris.'

'Christine!' roared Christine.

'Let me in, Christine. This is stupid. You know this is stupid. There is perfectly good food wasting down there.'

'Food. Food. Greedy pigs,' chanted Christine. 'Food, food, greedy pigs.'

Then Jo battered harder on the door and Christine could hear the lower tones of Max's voice. She scrabbled under her bed for her case and pulled back the lining to get at the razor she had taken all those months ago from her mother's bathroom cabinet.

It was so easy. The benediction of the cut, the flood of pain, then the dull throb of feeling and the healing pulse of blood. She waited till she was calm and went to pull back the door. She backed off and dropped onto the bed.

Jo grabbed a towel from the radiator and darted forward. 'Chris, what have you done? What have you done?'

Christine looked at her, eyes wide and empty. 'Christine,' she whispered. 'My name is Christine.'

After an overnight stay at the hospital she said she wouldn't go back with Jo and Max. 'The food's bloody awful,' she said as the social worker bundled her into her car.

'But Jo's food is lovely. Flora and Jenny love it.'

'They're greedy pigs,' said Christine. 'I want to go home to my Mum. You tell her I'll be a good girl. A good girl, if she'll let me come home.'

But her mother, hearing of the new episode, couldn't face having her.

After that, Christine was placed in another foster place from which she ran away back to her mother's home and barricaded herself in the bathroom. This time her mother sent for the social worker, who brought a female police officer with her. The two of them broke down the door. When they got into the tiny room Christine was sitting on the edge of the bath glaring at them. They looked round for blood and there was none. The room was shining bright, clean as always.

The social worker reached out for her and Christine flung out her arm against the woman, making her lose her balance and fall awkwardly between the toilet and the bath.

'Chris...' The police officer stepped over the social worker and took her by the shoulders. Christine kicked her on the shin and she swore, but held on tight.

In the end they hauled her, kicking and screaming, down the stairs and out of the door. All along the street the curtain twitched. The watchers saw how the child kept being pushed into the social worker's car before dodging straight out of the opposite door. Their curtains were opened wider when the child ran along the road, pursued by both the police officer and the social worker, to be hauled back and placed, this time, in the police car.

The social worker climbed in beside her and held both her hands. 'Chris... Chris... This is no good. No good at all.'

Christine looked her in the eyes. 'You can let me go now. I won't run. And Christine. Christine is my name.'

And that, she supposed, that must be the reason why she ended in the big house with the tall, locked gates. That was how she got to know Tigger. So it wasn't all bad. This place, called a *secure residential school* held some kids who had done very bad things like stealing and hurting people.

In some ways this place was better than Jo's house, because it was not so personal. You were not so much an audience for someone else's virtue. Here, you had to make your bed, keep your things tidy, turn up for meals. But these meals were crap-awful so you didn't have to be grateful. You turned up for lessons. These involved easy tasks—filling in messy moth-eaten workbooks—so that wasn't too bad.

They did Art on Fridays and, though she didn't show it, Christine thought that was OK. The bloke that did it didn't bother you too much. He put nice paints and pastels out for you and showed you how he did it. Then you messed about and did your own version.

She wrote dozens of letters to her mother, apologising, apologising for all the trouble and saying that she would never, never do any of that again. She wrote that Seamus had never really done anything. It was the first time she had mentioned Seamus. She watched the

49

post and after two weeks, when nothing came back, she broke a mirror and cut herself in the laundry, splashing blood over the clean sheets.

But in this place this caused no panic. Here they were geared for this kind of thing. The doctor stitched and bandaged her in the pristine surgery on the ground floor and tried to talk to her about why she did it. 'Drawing attention to yourself in this way will only harm yourself, Christine,' she said, putting her scissors back in the locked cabinet.

Christine frowned. 'Attention?'

'Why do you do it?'

She looked into the eyes of this woman. They were kind enough. 'Not about attention, It helps,' she said. 'It helps me.'

Boys coming back off weekend leave sometimes smuggled bottles of booze into the house. Beer. Wine. Martini was a favourite as it hit you faster. It was mostly boys who brought the booze in but the girls could get their hands on the stuff easily enough, in return for little favours.

Christine was not one for favours. She would not let the boys come near. After one or two scraps they didn't bother her. She was bigger and stronger than most of them: handy with her feet and her fists. It was Tigger who let them put their hands up her blouse and down her skirt. It was she who managed to get the polystyrene cups of booze which she shared with Christine. One day she vanished for a whole half an hour with one of the boys and came back into the room producing, with the flourish of a magician, a whole bottle of wine from under her cardigan . . .

They waited till after supper and retired to their room. There they turned their CD player right up. They danced and drank the wine very fast, finally falling on the bed in a stupor with the music still blaring. The night staff who came to tell them to turn their music off, saw the empty bottle and the state they were in and caused a ruckus. He gave them some bitter water to drink which made them sick, then made them drink pint glasses of water. Then he stood over them in their bedrooms while they stripped their beds and remade them with fresh sheets. Then he stood over them in the vast laundry while they bundled their sheets into one of the washers and turned it on.

Finally he watched them climb into bed and turned off the light. 'I'll talk to you in the morning. The first thing you will do is tell me where you got that stuff.'

But they never did.

*   *   *

Christine wrote to her mother again. This time she swore that Seamus had really been all right. That he had never hurt her. That she had been making it all up. She would come home and show her Mum how good she could

51

be. If only her Mum would forgive her.

This time a new social worker brought the letter back to her, opened, but sellotaped down again. 'I know it's hard, Chris, but your Mum's not been too well lately. She can't take all this pressure. Just leave off these letters for six months or so. Can you do that?'

'My name is Christine,' she growled. 'Christine.'

The woman's shoulders went up. 'No need to be like that Christine. How was I to know?'

That night, when Christine cut herself, she carved fine lines right down her forearms to the backs of her hands. It made a regular pattern. Straight lines, separated from each other but leading to the same place.

It took a lot of concentration to do the whole arm but she did it and in the maze of pain there was some relief. It was Tigger who found her and went screaming for help. It was Tigger who cried. No-one had ever cried for her before.

It was hospital this time, swirling lights, screaming siren, the lot. Tigger had wanted to get in the ambulance with her but they had held her back. In a woozy state, hurting like hell now the blood flow had stopped, the last thing Christine saw was Tigger's anxious little monkey face, wet with tears.

And that was the last time she saw Tigger for a long while. They wrote letters for a time. Tigger's letters were printed in block capitals.

There were only four of them. The last one was single line. *Mothers are fucking trouble an't they? They never listen do they? Yor ever lovin Tigger.*

*　　　*　　　*

Christine met Tigger again on her own second time inside. (For attacking a policeman again. Outside the pub, with too much vodka inside her. Tried to touched her up so she'd treated the joker to a black eye.) She spotted Tigger across the dining room and Tigger, who yelled 'Ye-es! Chris-tine!' And belted across the dining room to see her. They danced round and round, arms linked, under the eagle eye of the officers. Then they calmed down and sat at one of the tables side by side. Tigger, eighteen now, looked no different: slight, monkey-faced with that cute grin. They exchanged tales about coming up against the heavy-handed cops, running, doling, grafting booze and drugs..

'Still hurtin' yourself?' said Tigger, looking at Christine's bandages.

Christine pulled down the sleeves of her cardigan. 'It comes and goes,' she said.

They were called back to their cells then, and locked in till six. Christine lay on her bunk and ignored her pad-mate, thinking of the good times she and Tigger had in the residential school. Climbing up trees like lads. Smoking dope.

Playing snooker. Tigger, when she thought of it, had been the only one. The only one who ever knew her.

She knew she wouldn't see Tigger again till association the following night. The day stretched out to the length of a week. She cleaned up the narrow cell space with her pad-mate. Blankets folded military fashion. Walls. Sink. Lavatory bowl shining. Simple enough. The officer who inspected the cell, picked imaginary fluff off the top of the curtain rail and asked them if they'd bothered to clean that morning.

Christine's watch was still in Reception, so she didn't know the time. The day consisted of long stretches of sleep, breakfast and dinner on plastic plates, a visit from the teacher who took her through the usual questions and asked if she would like some cell studies. And more sleep.

Then, at last, tea and association. She looked eagerly round the long room for Tigger. She wasn't there. 'Where's Tigger?' she asked one of the women, a heavy woman who seemed to roll rather than walk about the place.

The woman winked, 'Yeh know that little pervert, then?'

'Pervert? Tigger?' Her fists curled. 'What yer bloody saying? She an't no pervert.'

'Not what I hear.'

'Well ye're goin' deaf then.'

'You watch it, or you'll get done yerself,' the woman growled.

'Done? They hurt her?'

54

The woman shrugged her massive shoulders. 'Wouldn't do it meself but ... what can the lass expect?'

Christine put her hand out to grasp the woman's arm and thought better of it. 'So what is it she's supposed to have done?'

'Only took some kids off, that she was baby sitting.'

'Took them off?'

'Aye. Drowned one of them in a river. Took the other for her boyfriend. One of the lasses just had a visit from her sister and she said it was in the paper.' The woman cupped her hand to take the ash dropping from her roll-up. 'Deserves anything she gets. Pervert.'

Christine opened her mouth to protest, then closed it. Then she said, 'Is she on the Wing?'

'Nah. She's down the bottom. Behind the door. They're keepin' her safe. But why they want to keep her safe, I don't fuckin' know. Deserves everything she gets.'

That night the noise, the shouting, the threats towards Tigger that were called through the bars made Christine's flesh creep. This set of women—tall, short, fat, thin—seemed the same as any group of women on any Wing, on any street. But at night when the shouting started, the voices hoarsened in the night air and joined together into a single wild roar of threat. A single beast.

Christine covered her head with the blanket, ignoring her pad-mate, who was with the others, shouting about just what she would do to anyone who hurt bairns, any fuckin' nonce who should be put down for her own good.

She lay awake all night and the next day when they were cleaning the cell her pad-mate told her to get out of bed and buck up. At this rate they would still be cleaning when the fucking officer came and anyway why was she working only with one hand? She reached over and took Christine's left hand and pushed back the sleeve of her sweatshirt. She dropped the hand. 'Fuckin' hell. What'yer at, lass?' She leaned over and pressed the alarm button. It took five minutes for an officer to get there.

'What is it?' The officer, Mrs Courtney, was a solid, capable woman who liked the job, but had learned early on to keep her face in a still mask.

'That lass!' The girl indicated Christine crouched up on the top bunk. 'Get her out of here. Look at her hand. She's fuckin' burnt herself.'

Mrs Courtney pulled at the hand and surveyed the mass of blisters. 'Well now, you'll get no tobacco after this, lady. Waste of a good fag.'

Christine was taken to the hospital wing to get the hand properly bandaged. The doctor talked to her. The nurse talked to her, but she would not talk back. She would tell them nothing. She was walking back to her room when she glimpsed Tigger, lounging pale-faced on a bed talking to the woman Christine recognised as a teacher. Tigger had a livid bruise on her cheek.

She stopped and leaned round the door. 'You

all right Tigger?' she said.

Tigger had smiled wanly, 'Surviving',' she said. 'Just about.'

The nurse behind Christine had dug her in the ribs. 'Come on, Cazalet. We haven't got all day. Don't waste time talking to that...'

After that day Tigger was shipped out and Christine never saw her again. Ever.

She found out six months later that Tigger had gone through all that for nothing. It was in the papers. Tigger got off on appeal because they'd found out she'd been fit up by the brother of the kids. But because of her record she seemed to be the likely one, the one that got arrested.

When she eventually got out Christine tried to find Tigger but she wasn't sure how you went about that and as time went by tried to get on with her own life. But she knew that of all the lessons Tigger had taught her the most important one was that you told no one anything. You kept your mouth shut about what you had done and you didn't tell them your proper name.

4 The Making of a Man

Ralph

The pit was the only thing for me, you know? Me, I'd be the first to admit we all have dreams of a life at sea, or serving king and country out there under the skies. Up there you savour the sunlight, even relish the rain lashing on your face. I do know of one or two lads that got out, up there into the day. One became a captain of a ship, another an inspector of police so there's no doubting the quality bred into Ashington men. Same in the War, the one that's just over. Five hundred Woodhorn men volunteered, though many never returned. They do say that the skills and strength of the mining men made a powerful contribution at the Front, some tunnelling under the guns of the Hun and blowing them to smithereens.

My own dreams of a life in the navy flew out of the window when stone fell on my father in this very pit. Death is in the way of things in the pit. Only two years ago thirteen men perished here in an explosion. It's just a year since my father was shot-firing a section of stone to clear the way back to the seam. Well, the same stone that he lovingly drilled and fed with gunpowder crashed down on him and his marrow, his best mate. Neither of them survived the two hours it took to carry them out-bye, twelve men taking turns at this arduous task.

So, though I was a good scholar and liked school I had to leave and come here to work at this same pit. My mother told me this was necessary: the only way to hang onto the colliery house that shelters her and me and my brothers and sisters: eight of us in all. At first, being so young they kept me on the surface, picking stone on the screens. But I always knew the only place for man's work is down below. That's where the better money is. And better money I need because the pittance I got from picking stones on the screens has been barely kept my Mam and my brothers and sisters from the workhouse.

There is this special language. *Pig's tail rope clip, ham bone rope clip*, I am to learn about these things seeing as on-setting is to be my first job underground. And I'll learn about picks, shovels, drills and props, seeing as I am set to be a real pitman and maybe even end up as a hewer, like my Uncle Jonna.

After what happened to my father, maybe I should have avoided the pit altogether, but this dark place pulls you in. *It pulls you* like the continuous chain that pulls the tubs out-bye to the shaft-bottom, where I stand with the on-setter learning my job. Here the on-setter unclips each tub and pushes it into the cage before he sets the empty tub back on the chain. *Back on the chain*, so it can be dragged back to the straight, so the pony putters can take it down the narrow ways to the conveyor laden with the coal gouged out by the hewer and brought out from the coalface. On that straight the fillers shovel the coal into the empty tubs which are hauled on by the chain. *Hauled on* back to us at bank so we can unhook them and push then on so the *rolley man* can get them into waiting cage and send them up the shaft to the day. *So the pit pulls you in: a never ending chain.*

Last night, knowing that on-setting will be a different kettle of fish from picking coals on the surface, I make sure I get to my bed early. Still, my mother has to shake me hard to wake me and drag me out of bed at half past one. It's still pitch black outside. My bait-tin and bottle of water sit on the table beside a steaming cup of tea and a thick jam sandwich. My Uncle Jonna, my father's brother, is crouched on his hunkers by the fire, a pot mug of tea in his hand. Even crouching, he dwarfs the room with his size. He nods, 'Man's shift today, Ralphy, nee lass's job up top for you today.'

I lean down to lace up my father's boots, taken from his very feet after they carted his body home on an old door. My mother said we couldn't afford to waste them. His lamp too, stands ready for me on the table. His coat is on

60

the peg by the door. Beside that hangs my new cloth cap with its steel peak. Mam was down Ashington Co-op buying it just yesterday. When she came back she stood it me in front of the mirror and jammed it down on my curls. She stared at me through the mirror, not a tear in her eye and said, 'Noo hinney,' she says. 'Mind you dinnet lose it. It cost good money.'

Jonna

Our young Ralph's making a good fist of this, walking down the pit road alongside me. He clumps along in his too-big boots, his hands deep the pockets of the coat that still carries the scent of my brother. Other pitmen join us at the street-ends, trickles turning to streams, then becoming a river as we reach the pit yard.

'Now, Jonna!'

'Now Joss!'

'Now, young Ralph.'

Many of them know the lad's my brother's son and show their respect for the boy's heritage with a nod.

'Now Jonna!' My marrow Harold Crow joins us at the gate and reminds me to talk to the deputy about the problem of the tub of ours that had small coal as well as roundies and showed us short on last payday. It needs sorting. I explain all this to Ralph as me and Harold collect our tokens from the Time Office. 'They don't credit you if it's mixed load, son. Dig a score of tubs

and get paid for nineteen! But we know it was all good stuff. We think mebbe the lad on filling got careless and now we lose out. We look out for each other down the pit, but in the end you have to look after yourself. Everybody has a living to make after all.' The lad looks at us, taking it all in.

I say to him. 'Me and Harold'll have to check it out with the deb'ty and if he's no help I'll try the check-weighman, who has more clout. Aa'll not be cheated out of me just pay.'.

I introduce Ralph to young Frankie Cornish who's the on-setter and will show him the ropes in that job. Frankie has been told by the over-man so he knows all about it. The two lads shake hands but don't say much. There'll be plenty time for them to talk as the long shift plays itself out. Frankie has his marrow Kit Slater helping him today but he's to be a pony- putter tomorrow. Like his Dad he's mad about the galloways. So our Ralphy'd better learn sharpish.

I have to stoop when I get into the crowded cage and pull our Ralphy in tight beside me. Three men are crouched on their hunkers in the corner so as to make more space for the rest of us. A few of the men murmur a greeting to Ralph but don't mention his father. That wouldn't do, with us on the way down.

Frankie takes Ralph in hand at the shaft bottom so me and Harold can get on and check with the deputy at his kist, about that disqualified tub. He makes a note about this in his book and *we take his direction about our work this shift. It's a good walk in-bye to the working. We hitch a lift on a pony-limber but still it takes the best part of an hour to reach to our work through the dim galleries.. We have to walk the last bit half-crouching, squeezing our way past the conveyor that will carry the coal down to the straight for the putters to fill.*

According to the deputy we're to undercut this section ready for the shot-firer, so he can do his bit for us to win the coal. Our place is just one stall down from the one we cut last week. It's a good run of coal but crucifyingly low. Three foot to get in, but as low as two and a half foot where we're hewing. Cramped working. I can only use my half-pick in there. Harold's's not so happy in narrow seams these days because of his arthritis. But he's a prodigious worker and even keeps up with me. I know, though, that the day will come when he won't be able to keep up and I'll be forced to work with another lad. But there'll never be a marrow like Frankie.

We'll fill the undercut coal ourselves onto the conveyor but when the shot-firer brings down the section of the seam we'll need one of the filling lads to help. The fillers are canny lads but can be careless sometimes, hence my problem last week.. I like to keep an eye on the filling myself, and hook on my own token. But last week I missed the mistake, being distracted by a lad in the next stall whose pick head had fallen off. I stepped to one side to help him secure it again.

63

A hewer needs his pick. As well as this, a hewer needs explosive strength and a real knowledge of the coal and how it lies in the seam. Working in the half-dark he needs to know how best to coax it out of its ancient nest where it has lingered for a million years.

Of course there are mechanical coal cutters around now, with steam drivers and longer conveyors than we have in our narrow seam. There's no filling of tubs in a narrow seam like ours, I'm telling you. One time it was all ponies, now these new things are coming in, to make the job easier.

But it is just as hard as it ever was, to hew coal in a narrow seam. So this morning when bait time comes around me and Frankie are pleased to get settled down on our crackets and get out our bait. We turn off our lamps to rest our eyes, letting the pit go back to its normal darkness as we talk on. We talk together and call out to the men in the next stall.

The crack's all right.

The subject of John Snaith comes up. He's just back from the War and they thought him fit to work underground. But on his first shift back he fought and screamed as the cage dropped in the shaft. The banksman sent him straight back up into the day. It turns out that the poor lad was trapped in a collapsing trench in Ypres and has nightmares. He works on the Co-op waggon now, delivering meat out Newbiggin and Lynemouth. Not man's work if you ask me.

Ralph

'Howwa Ralphy, coom on Kit, time for wor bait.'

At bait time the grind and pull of the chain stops and the cages are still. A rippling quiet settles through the galleries and the sound of urgent movement is replaced by the snuffle of ponies, a man whistling a tune and a low indifferent hum of men's voices. The mine, like its men, is at rest.

It's a great relief to obey Frankie Cornish and sit by the wall with him and his marrow, Kit, the one who's soon to become a pony putter. After all these hours of work I'm speechless with exhaustion and defeated by the grinding continuity of the job. I open my bait box and out of it comes the sweet smell of my mother's kitchen. I have to tell you I am near to tears. But I take a great bite of the jam sandwich and its sweetness is a comfort.

Frankie's not as old as Uncle Jonna, maybe only twenty six, and not so serious. But he's wise in the ways of the pit and has been showing me the ropes in more ways than one this morning. I've learned how to catch the tubs as they swing round then loosen the clips, push them to the rolley-man and lift on the empties. There's more to it than you'd think. Your fingers can get trapped and the laden tubs are heavy and you've got to make haste as more tubs are coming up. The rope goes on and on giving up its glittering black cargo into our hands.

Frankie says it's best to keep going, steady as you go. One time I was dragging them up too fast and he says, 'Woah man. Steady as ych go. Only way of doin' this job, marrer. Steady as yeh go.'

Easy for him to say. His 'steady' is my top speed.

When we sit with our bait he asks me if I'm as good a footballer as my uncle and have I tried my hand at snooker as it's a great game for a man with a good eye. Then without waiting for an answer he asks me if I've been to the Co-op Hall where you can see moving pictures on some weekends. 'Man. It's magic. Syem as the real thing. I'm tellen yeh!'

Then he leaves me in peace and talks to Kit about his leeks and a new racing pigeon he has acquired. A real flyer, apparently. Kit talks about a pig he's feeding up that'll get fat on air and potato peelings. Then they start to talk of the pit owners and how they profit from the sweat of the working man's brow. Then there's this new influenza that's raging around. According to the paper it was brought home by the men returning from The War. This leads to talk of friends who did not return from the trenches and lie, nurtured forever now by the foreign earth. Funny that. Those men lying out there under the earth, having worked here under this earth here when they were just my age.

Then Kit starts on about the ponies that he calls *gallowas*. Seems his father was a horse-keeper who loved his ponies, before he died one day when the cage stopped short and he stepped on air, only to be crushed then by the cage. 'My Da fed his gallowas, bliddy nurtured'm, washed the dust from their eyes and their thick coats. Sometimes he even stayed ower a shift to nurse one through some sickness. Mad for them, he was.'

'So what happens when they die?' I ask.

Kit to me. 'Why, son, if the poor buggers get sick, like, they're sent up into the day and the slaughterer gets them for dog-meat. My old man had a favourite, a nice old girl called Lil, that died down here in a blast. Had to send her up wedged in a tub.'

I take another large bite of my jam and bread to force down the lump that seems to have gathered in my throat. Frankie looks at me hard then and talks about how in one gallery they us a water sump like a kind of swimming bath and swim the ponies through to get them clean. Then we hear the sound of whistles in the tunnel and the chain shudders into action as though it has a life of its own and is waking from sleep.

Jonna

We've cleared the undercut now and the shot-firer's drilling his holes. He's a big lad, plays goalkeeper in our team and they say they're gunna test him for Newcastle. To get down into the seam to do his job he has to fold himself up like a concertina, his thick, bony knees almost up to his chin. He blows his whistle and we all retire. He's a brave man. I've known more than one man killed on this job. Look at my own brother.

The explosion crackles through the galleries and there's a kind of grating <u>whoosh</u> and we know the coal's down. The whole seam appears to lift and settle itself and me and Harold get down to do our part of the job.

Ralph

The second part of the shift goes much more quickly than the first. From time to time the low crack of an explosion echoes through the galleries right down to where we are setting on. The steady delivery of tubs slows and near the end of the shift, as I unclip and heave the very last tub it nearly runs over my foot. My father comes into my mind again. That last morning he went out to the pit in these very boots. They clattered down the back yard and I imagined them striking sparks on the stone flags. This morning it was the boots on my feet striking sparks off the flags with my mother standing at the gate, arms folded till I vanish into the dark.

The shift ends. The last tubs are on their way up now and we relax a bit, stretch our shoulders, rub our tired faces with our coal blackened hands. The hewers, putters, drivers and drawers hurry to the shaft bottom in large numbers. There is noise and eager confusion as they push through, desperate to get up into the day. My uncle and his marrow ride in on one of the last tubs before the chain stops. His face, streaked and weary, breaks into a smile when he sees me. 'Now, Ralphy! Good shift?'

'Aye. All right.' I know better than to tell him how I really feel, how exhausted I am. The men stand back to let the boys go first up into the cage but I stay by my uncle Jonna's side. Then it's my turn to be drawn up in the cage squashed in with Frankie and Jonna and the other men. I stand silent sucking my sore knuckles, bearing my aching muscles in silence.

My uncle stands, head bent, like the other men in the cage. He carries his two picks—one short handled, one long—under one arm. He takes his picks home with him and keeps them sharp himself, not trusting the pick-man here. He's said to me more than once that a man is only as good as the tools he carries.

We press our way out of the cage and surge along the gantry and down the steps to where the men are waiting for the next shift.

As we make our way across to the cabin to give in our tokens the wheel is still creaking, swooping to collect more or its own. The new men are standing and sitting around, easy in the afternoon sunshine even though there is a sharp wind coming from the sea. Their faces are clean, their hair brushed under their caps. Seeing them, my heart lifts inside me. My own shift's done. I'm going home and within the hour I'll be sitting in the tin bath before the blazing fire and my mother will wash my back. Then I will sit at her table and eat her knuckle broth and mashed potatoes. My mouth waters.

I can feel Uncle Jonna's gaze, his eyes narrow in his blackened face. 'Whey, Ralph, your mother won't recognise you as the syem lad. She sent out a boy and there comes home a man.'

Then we turn away from the pit with its gantry and its turning wheels and, shoulder to shoulder, we set out down the pit-road for the long walk through the high waste mountains to our hard-won hearth and home.

5 Married Life

Imogen Smith was married to Freddie for thirty-eight years and twenty seven days. Freddie established himself as the boss on the day of their engagement, when he told Imogen she must wear a blue dress, not the white dress she had carefully and joyfully chosen for their wedding. After all, pressed the earnest Freddie, she had admitted losing her virginity at the age of fourteen to the boy who delivered Tizer to her mother's house on Saturdays. 'You told me that,' he said. 'The second time we went out together.'

'You were like a dog at a bone,' she said fondly. 'Getting that out of me.'

Freddie liked to make his own wine and took an interest in the local community action committee that focussed on the slowing of traffic and the provision of bicycle lanes throughout the city. But his greatest passion was for the acquisition of books. He bought them by the yard, by the mixed box and in singles. The first thing he did when they moved into their nice semi-detached was to build ceiling-high shelves in the recesses in their small sitting room. By their second wedding anniversary this was not enough, so he began to build shelves in every room and corridor, in every nook and cranny, over every door and window to accommodate them. The shelves were very well built. He proudly called them 'over-engineered' and said the house would fall down before the shelves sagged. Even the toilet had its built-in library, although the texts on those shelves were appropriately short. Still the books came in. In the end most of the shelves were stacked at double-depth. Imogen countered her friends' looks of astonishment by saying—they never knew whether she was being proud or ironic—'Freddie can locate each and every one of them. He doesn't need a card index.'

Next to hoarding books Freddie loved walking on the moors and climbing mountains. By dint of his careful planning and methodical use of holidays and long breaks he and Imogen managed to tackle nearly every long walk and most of the high mountains in England and Wales. They didn't tackle Lands End to John O'Groats because Freddy thought that would be showing off.

From being elegant and willowy Imogen became tough and wiry. It was when she was fifty-three, though, that she started to have trouble with her left heel. She went to the doctor.

'When does it occur, Mrs Smith?' he said. 'This pain?'

'Well,' she said, 'the first twelve miles are fine. Then the pain kicks in.'

The doctor laughed in her face and waved

her away, saying he had sick people to deal with.

Freddie also loved jazz with a passion, so they got into the habit of travelling to concerts in distant towns, sometimes taking in a mountain on the way. He collected records as well as books, so as they travelled they combed boot sales, junk shops and markets in search of early versions of the jazz greats. He developed a complex reference matrix for his records which meant he could put his hand on the most obscure track on the rarest record in ten seconds.

After her marriage Imogen trained as a teacher and in time, became the youngest head-teacher in the region. She was humorous, mild and disciplined at the same time and made a very good head teacher. This, of course, was as nothing compared with Freddie's achievements as a senior dental technician in a very important practice. He had made moulds for the most significant mouths in the region. 'It gives me a take on these people,' he would say. 'Everyone has their weak spot.'

As well as working, collecting books and records and climbing mountains, in time Freddie and Imogen had three children in various sizes who covered the range of gender identity. These youngsters were generally little trouble and progressed easily through school and university, to safe but interesting jobs and safe but interesting partners and eventually moved away to pursue their own lives in different parts of the country, Occasionally the whole family would get together for a good climb or a nice, long, challenging walk. They continued this tradition even when grandchildren came along. Freddie was driven to design Class A and Class B walks to accommodate all abilities. Imogen, although capable of Class A walks, always joined the Class B walkers, her grandchildren. Her children applauded this motherly gesture and strode off with their father and the more capable spouses.

After her contretemps with the doctor over her foot Imogen enrolled with the Open University. She opted for a course in Soviet Literature and fell in love with her summer school tutor, Tommy Smythson, a rather lanky man who was ten years her junior. The two of them had many intense conversations where the intellectual bordered on the erotic. He told her she was the very image of the elegant Anna Akhmatova, his literary obsession. Imogen was in sixth heaven for a while but was crestfallen at the end of the second summer school when Tommy broke off their relationship. When pressed, he admitted to some confusion about his own gender identity and baulked at the final consummating step in their relationship. Above the waist was far enough for him.

A rather frustrated, Imogen returned from

that Summer School to find an old friend from school on her doorstep. Imogen blinked a little at the sight of this person because now her friend Beth had transformed herself to Bernard. He sat foursquare in Imogen's kitchen smoking his pipe, demonstrating that he had no problem at all with his gender identity. After that visit the two of them corresponded, became confidants and something of a strength to one another..

When he reached fifty-eight, Freddie started to slow down a bit and Imogen went trekking in India on her own. She met interesting people there from many different countries. Her favourite person was Mamie Cottrell of Colorado Springs who walked up hills in high-heeled shoes. Imogen's new friends considered her very special and treated her tenderly. After six weeks she came back with a notebook full of contact addresses all over the world and some wonderful photographs. Freddie barely glanced at them. He was not interested in these wonders, that he had not witnessed. After all had had just acquired a first edition R C Hutchinson in an Edinburgh Oxfam shop. He gloated about it to Imogen. Now he had every edition of every one of Hutchinson's masterpieces he could relax.

By this time Imogen had so many contacts that she was writing letters every day and considering the possible benefit of a computer and the instant comforts of email. She was so busy with her correspondence that she welcomed an offer of early retirement when her education authority merged several schools. Retirement gave her time to write her letters and visit some of her nearer contacts, including Bernard who had become a wildlife warden for the forestry commission and had a companion, a man much younger than him who was a wonderful cook and gardener.

Three days after his fifty-ninth birthday Freddie, unfortunately, drowned in Huddersfield Canal, having lost his footing on a narrow path on his way to a back-street bookshop. His funeral was crowded with all the generations of his family and many of Imogen's friends. One by one, her daughters and daughters-in-law urged her to live near them so that her grandmotherly wisdom would be on hand for them and their children.

Imogen said to each of them that she appreciated their kind offers and she would think about their suggestions. Then, after a month had passed she sold Freddie's valuable books and records to collectors, burned the uncollectable ones, and sold the house. She made a good profit on the books but had to reduce the price of the house somewhat, because the dismantling of the over-engineered shelves meant that the interior of the house had to be completely re-plastered.

Homeless now, she made a pilgrimage

around England visiting her children and grandchildren. Then she gathered all her resources and bought a first-class airline ticket to America, where she acquired a well-equipped liberty vehicle and set off to visit Mamie Cottrell in Colorado. The two of them had a plan to take a trip up through the Rocky mountains to Canada, a trip they had dreamed of while walking in India.

After that Imogen thought she would take things as they came and begin to live her own life.

6 Sandy Cornell

I met Sandy Cornell at the worst time of my life and in retrospect she saved my life. That I survived to live now, that I have children and grandchildren, that I have endured and enjoyed the adventures of my life is down to her.

Sandy and I went to this very modern school with plate glass windows, a state-of-the-art-school, a brave-new-world-school, an envy-of-the-district school. It was a very working class school, but still a wish-we-were-Eton school. It was a wearing-uniform school, a teachers-wearing-gowns school, a doing-your-homework school, a thank-god-we-won-the-war school.

There was no refuting the fact that I was clever when I arrived there. Placed straight into the A stream, I was seventh in the class which meant seventh in the whole district where this was the best school. Sporting dirty hands and scruffy clothes I was still a natural; words and ideas entered through my eyes and ears and found valid connections in the universe of my brain. Success in English and French were underpinned by voracious reading of unsuitable material like comics and salacious novels as well as the decent stuff. Achievements in History and Geography were underpinned by intense discussions at home where, for hours at a time, my mother and I would forget that the fire had gone out or there was little for supper and talk. At first, with such excellent home tutoring I could spin ideas, spew words out on the page in some order and get good marks at school.

Scruffy and unkempt though I was, I was taken up by Alma Simpson, an outstandingly pretty girl who was flirtatious and popular. She mesmerised me. I felt warm in her presence. Later, when our ways parted, I came to notice that she always took up with outsiders: people who could worship gratefully at her shrine, people who, in contrast with her, were scruffy or ugly or in some other way misbegotten. She shone in such company.

As time went on in this school the most profound feeling I experienced was fear. I was afraid of the teachers: alien creatures whose faces were hard and unreadable, who would punch you and flick you with impunity, and call you by your surname or merely with the epithet *girl*! I was afraid of the boys who were bouncy and brave, whose word for sanitary towels was *jam-rags* and who called you names, cornering you with their energy, so that you wished profoundly to be invisible and began to walk around as though you were. Most of all I was afraid of the wall of work that, though not difficult to me, piled up and remained undone because I went home from school to brood and sleep in my misery, dreaming of invisibility.

My friend Alma, who smirked and looked at her nails when the boys bawled and ragged me, had a miraculous answer for the undone work. No need to worry, she said. 'You know, when the teacher asks you to call out your mark? They don't check. Just say any mark. Not too high. Somewhere in the middle. I'm always doing it.'

So I tried her miracle method and, unlike her, was discovered in my fraud. It was the most miserable time ever in my life. I was made to feel as guilty as if I had murdered someone. The headmaster, stout and smelling of sweat, stood there on the stage in front of the whole school, swinging his spectacles on his forefinger. 'I can't fight liars,' he said. 'You know who you are. I know who you are. I can't fight liars.'

I stood there frozen, cloaked in my invisibility and watched him swing those spectacles, his little finger daintily in the air.

After that incident I stayed away from school for nearly a term. I wrote my own sickness letters. Nobody seemed to notice. The school didn't notice. My mother didn't notice. I was in my uniform when she went to work, I was in uniform when she returned home and flopped on the couch in exhaustion. For me this proved I must have attained invisibility. I think now that if cutting had been even conceivable then, as it is now, I would have cut myself. If I'd had the means, I would have ended it all, made myself invisible.

As it was, I knew I had to return to school, to become visible again. More than once I got as far as the big school doors and retreated. One day, when I tried returning to school, I remember looking at the reflection of the dark winter sky in the plate glass windows and feeling that the inside of this place with its chairs and books and nipping teachers was an illusion, a dream. For a full minute I was in suspension. I could not go in and I could not go back. The thought chiseled itself into my brain that I had choices. I could go inside, or I could go back home and go to sleep. Or, I could walk right down the lane to the river and walk in up to my neck, arms out like Jesus.

No. I would go in, into the school. One foot after another I forced myself forward. Then I rushed forwards and pushed the door hard and it swung back against a stout body. The headmaster's currant black eyes glittered. His salmon steak cheeks flushed. 'What? What? You girl. What're you doing?' Spit clung to the corner of his mouth.

I tucked in my chin. 'Coming into school, sir.'

'You've been out?'

He smelled of old cheese and toilets.

'Yes sir.'

'It's not allowed.'

Sweat was running down his temple into his

ear.

'I know sir.'

'Why have you been out?'

'I been home, sir.'

'It's not allowed.'

'I know sir.'

'So, why did you go home?'

'I went to put the light under the boiler sir. For the washing.'

'Why? That's your mother's job. To light the boiler.'

'My mother's at work, sir.'

'At work?'

'At the factory. Doesn't get home till five. Then she does the washing, it being Monday.'

A long unbearable silence. Then he sniffed. 'Don't do it again, girl. It's not allowed.'

'No sir.' I looked for a clear way round him but he stood in such a way that I had to squeeze past him. Then I walked right through the school to the back entrance, ran home and lay on the couch thinking what a mistake it had been to try, to try to get back through the glass door.

I did go back, after the long summer holiday, at the beginning of the new school year. The summer had been a rest from the worry and I managed to forced myself back to school properly. In this new world Alma Simpson had taken on a new friend, a whey-faced gangly girl with a receding chin and bottle-bottomed glasses. Beside this girl Alma looked even more enchantingly pretty. I realized then that, as Alma's scruffy sidekick, I had been used in the same way.

That term, in an accident of placing, I sat beside Sandy Cornell who had skin like a peach and was six foot tall: a dreamy, willowy flower. She was always neat in her uniform and had new pens, pencils and protractors at the beginning of each term. I finally emerged from my fog to notice that, rather than the quiet person I'd thought she was, Sandy was kind, funny and laid back. She made me laugh. We walked with linked arms. I was welcomed into her cosy house by her domesticated, comfortable mother and her hardworking father. At weekends I would retrieve the deposit on returnable bottles just to get the bus fare to visit that family with its predictable routines, its ordinary down-to-earth humour.

Sandy Cornell was the first—although not the last—person I ever met who used irony as an everyday tool. Untroubled by the fact that she was not overwhelmingly clever she was comfortable in her skin and was never a target for the exquisite boy-cruelty that had haunted me for two years. She smiled ironically at those monsters behind their backs, looked dreamily down at them from a great height. She was obviously no pleasure as a target.

By some miracle, when I was at Sandy's side, the taunts stopped. The fear that had haunted me in my time there receded and my cleverness wound itself into a rope-ladder that helped me climb out of the pit I'd dug for myself. Now I was able to go on and live a visible life.

To bring this all up to date: something strange happened just this week. From the spinning planet of my adult life I see a notice in the paper declaring that my old school is celebrating its fiftieth anniversary. I decide to pay it a visit. With dozens of other pilgrims I make my way through the bring-and-buy and the icecream stalls, up the steps, (past the disco-desk providing music for brave salsa-dancers up on a dais), into the school.

Of course the place seems smaller. The vast reaches of the main hall where the headmaster swung his glasses have receded: its floor is shrunk now by two generations of tramping feet. The corridors are narrower. The staircases—scenes of torment—are mean and undistinguished. The classrooms are familiar, although the plate glass windows are dusty. Standing in the middle of what was the French room, fear inhabits me again, like a dormant virus nudged into life. My blood runs hot then very cold. Choking for breath I hurry back through huddles of benign, nostalgic strollers to escape this hellish place.

'Funny thing, that, a headmaster running a disco,' a middle-aged man ahead of me murmurs to his wife.

On the steps of the school stands a man

running a disco desk. He's wearing a straw hat and a bow tie and has the look of an extra in a Tennessee Williams play. I go to stand beside him but he does not look up from his turntable. I cough. 'Are you the head teacher here?'

'Mmm.' He pushes a lever.

'I was here at this school fifty years ago,' I say. 'When it was brand new. I was a pupil here.'

He murmurs something but still he does not look up.

I persist. 'I can see you that are not in the least interested in me,' I say. I will *not* be invisible.

Now the headteacher looks up, his face bland, his eyes cold, 'I have to do this. I have to run this desk. The dancers need the music.' His spectacles hang on a leather thong round his neck.

My eye lights on some boys, lounging sullen-faced in the plate glass doorway I pushed through all those years ago. Their greedy eyes watch the head teacher's every movement as he handles the state of the art equipment. He could put them in charge of the sound desk but he doesn't. He is happy where he is, presiding over the disco. His head goes down again and I make my way steadily, steadily down the steps, through the crowds round the bring-and-buy and the ice cream stalls to my car. It is brand new, state of the art; like the disco set-up. As

85

I put my car into gear I think for the first time in many years about Sandy Cornell. I hope she is well and happy. She deserves to be. As I say, she saved my life.

6 The Paperweight

Donny rubbed the cottage window and peered in into the tiny cluttered room. He could make out a heavy man with a shock of grey hair slumped in a chair by a flickering fire. The man was reading and smoking a cigarette and he was clearly on his own.

'Oh yes!' Donny grinned to himself and splashed his way round to the front door. He banged on the door with the flat of his hand.

'Coming! Coming!' A growling voice.

The heavy wooden door swung open suddenly. Donny lurched inwards, knocking into the man who was standing behind it. 'Steady! Steady!' The man clutched Donny's shoulder and held him at arms length. He smelled of tobacco and dust. 'Drowned rat, is it?' he said. 'You'd better come in.'

He pulled the boy inside and banged the door shut against the driving rain. The house had no hall or vestibule. They were standing in the room with the lamp: living room and kitchen all in one. Donny put down his rucksack and stood very still. Then he shook his head hard and rain from his long hair sprayed like silver and sizzled when it reached the fire.

'You'd better get that coat off, son, before you flood the place.' The man's deep voice did not sound local.

Donny slipped out of his treasured military coat and the man reached forward to take it. From long habit Donny ducked, then handed it to the man, who carefully arranged it on a chair by the window. He reached down a towel from an overhead rail and thrust it towards the boy. 'Dry yourself off son,' he said, 'I need to know me what you're doing out here, in the middle of no-where.' He nodded towards a upright chair standing by the fire. 'Sit down there and I'll get you a drink.' He moved towards the draining board, rinsed out a cup and clicked on a kettle. He moved with a degree of grace for such a heavy man. Donny thought perhaps he might have done some boxing at some time. A long time ago, it must be, though. He was carrying a lot of weight now and was no spring chicken.

Donny looked around the room. Comfortable chairs with worn covers. Table covered with papers and books. Discarded cups and crumbs all over the place. No photographs. Not one. Bloke lives on his own, he thought. He spied a silver jug among plates on a narrow dresser. Not bad.

He leaned over, picked up a paperweight holding down a pile of papers on a shelf, weighing it in his hands: two butterflies suspended in glass: one large one small; one brown, one yellow; one with wings spread, one with wings folded.

The man took it from him and replaced it on the dresser. 'Strange thing isn't it? Half thing of beauty, half method of singular destruction. Butterflies are real, you know. It was a present from my wife to my old man. My ex-wife that is.' He handed Donny a mug of tea and a plate with a pie on it. 'You must be hungry, I'm having one myself.' he said. 'Must be all of two hours since I ate.'

Bit of a pig, then, thought Donny. Doesn't take care of himself. He flexed his own shoulder muscles while he chewed his pie. Being inside taught you to take care of yourself. Good insurance if you wanted to survive.

The man took his own plate and sat on the other, more comfortable chair. 'So, son, what *are* you doing out here in the wilds on the wettest night of the year?'

Donny looked at him carefully and decided the truth might just work. 'I hitched a lift with this bloke and he tried it on with us. You know. Perve stuff. And when I clocked him one he dumped me up here on the moors.'

'Bad luck, that.' The man bit into his pie. 'Joss, by the way. Joss Cannon. You?' He spoke with his mouth full, spraying crumbs.

'Donny Hammond.'

Joss nodded, shaking his jumper so the crumbs dropped to the floor. . 'So, my guess is you're running away from... something?'

'Nah. Running towards. Trying to get to

London to see my sister. She has this job lined up. So she says.'

'And you've no money for a bus?'

'Not true. I got this bit of money. Thought hitching would save it for later. When I get to London.' His eyes left Joss and slid around the room and stopped again at the silver jug. 'I'll need funds. I'm gunna pay my way with my sister.'

A log in the hearth crackled and split, sending sparks up the chimney.

Joss brushed more crumbs off his shirt with his hand. 'You've been away haven't you, son? Inside?'

Donny clapped his hand on his forehead. 'Jeez! I forgot to get me tattoo lasered.' He was feeling warmer, easier now. 'So! Are you the filth?' He put down his mug and flexed his knuckles. 'You got the look, come to think of it.'

Joss shook his head. 'Army, then probation, now retired.'

'Would 'a thought it'd suit you. Probation. Easy money, that. You get sacked, like?'

'No. Got sick of chasing rubbish paper and bad people.' Joss settled back into his chair. 'I have to say I'm pleased to see you though, here, tonight..'

Donny sat up straight. 'Hey! You're not pervy like that freakin' driver, are you?'

Joss laughed. 'No chance. Just sick of my own company, to be honest.'

90

'So why're you hidin' away here in the wilds? You gotta be a volunteer, not a victim.'

Joss lumbered across to the window and peered out at the storm. He spoke with his back to Donny. 'Old story, son. I mislaid a job, mislaid a wife who said I cared too much, mislaid a house and mislaid a life. Nowhere to go so I came back here to my Dad's old place to mooch about a bit. Trying to write things and failing. Been here two months. But now, like I say, I'm sick of my own company.' He came back to his seat and reached for another pie. 'Pig sick,' he added thoughtfully.'

'You'll get fat, mate,' said Donny.

'I am fat, didn't you notice?' said Joss. He looked around the room. His eye lingered on the silver jug. 'So! You thinking of robbing any of this stuff? That silver tea jug's worth a few bob. And that fishing rod's worth hundreds. And there's forty five quid in my wallet in that drawer.'

Donny was suddenly angry. He scowled. 'You jokin' ancher? I just got out. Like I said, I'm on my way to my sister's. I ain't going back to any of those places.'

Joss sat back in his chair looking at Donny in silence. Donny met his gaze then dragged his eyes away. He put his plate and cup on the table. 'So, is this where I tell you my troubles and you tell me to mend my ways, forget the past, live for the future and be a good boy?'

'No son, it's not. To be honest I'm not that

interested in your troubles.' Joss waved a hand dismissively. 'Any more than I would burden you with mine. And I've got plenty.'

'You got troubles? *You?*'

Joss grunted. 'Plenty. Small matter of this wife of mine, who thinks I care too much and has teamed up with a chap not much older than you, in the house that I bought. And then there's the other small matter of a doctor warning me that if I don't mend my habits I'll be dead within a year.' He paused. 'Makes you think, son, somebody saying that.' He leaned over and threw a log on the fire which dimmed, then flamed up again.

'Bloody hell, mate! You're not thinking of topping yourself?' the words shot from Donny's mouth before he could stop them. He closed his eyes. 'I seen it, man! There was this lad on my wing that topped himself. Gruesome! Don't do it mate.' He opened his eyes and glared angrily at his host.

Joss waited a full second before shaking his head. 'Course not! I'd never do any such thing. Not now.' He paused. 'Now then, son. Are you any kind of hand at poker?'

'Am I! Did little else in the hostel, mate. Against the rules, but you know how it is.'

Joss rubbed his hands together. 'Right! You and I will have a few hands of poker, enjoy a good night's sleep, and I'll drive you to the station in the morning. You can have that money in my wallet for the fare to London.

And you can take that silver jug with you. And you can even have the butterfly paperweight if you promise not to bang me on the head with it.' He hefted it in his hand and peered into it. 'Suspended animation. You and me in there, son. Held in suspended animation. Time we broke out, don't you think?'

He stood up, reached into a drawer, pulled out a deck of cards and started to shuffle them.

Donny stared at him suspiciously. 'Wassa matter? Why're you being so goody goody? So bloody Mother Teresa?'

Joss pulled a small table between them and started to deal the cards. 'Tell you the truth, Donny, up till the moment I saw you there, dripping like a drowned dog on my mat I thought that not a single soul gave a toss about me and no-one would ever miss me.'

Donny grinned. 'I knew it!' He picked up his hand of cards. 'You were gunna top yourself!'

'Sensitive soul, aren't you? Whatever.' Joss paused. 'Anyway, when I saw you dripping on my doormat I just wanted to laugh. You made me want to laugh. All that ...funny stuff, all that darkness that's been haunting me for weeks...' He made a clumsy job of lighting a cigarette. '...Well, all that stuff just fell off me like a pealed skin. Can't tell you why. But I feel clean and clear now. Clean and clear..'

'You're mad, man!' said Donny, shaking his

head. 'Freaking mad.'

'Takes one to know one.' Joss picked up his hand. 'Now then, son, your drop I think?'

8 Passion

When they started talking about the final closing of the pit, weeping and wailing like they did, I thought about another thing that was vanishing—the feeling men have for each other, the friendship so special it has always had a special word. 'He's me *marrer*,' they'd say. Or 'I worked *marrers* with him ten years'. The real word was marrow. But they said *marrer*. The word meant more than *workmate* or *friend*. It involved a unique mutuality, humour, dependability and trust, it has shared history and the woven texture of risky experience.

Like a marriage.

My Joe would not like me talking like this. That's the thing, of course. They never do talk about it. Especially not to each other.

You can see a grotesque cartoon of this feeling when you see a documentary on the telly about, say, football fans. Here are these big men, broad shoulders, thickened waists, drawing hard on their cigarettes, waxing sentimental about their team, using playground pet names like Makka, Gazza, Smiler or Tommo—a way of naming echoed on the sports pages. This way of naming is a false signal of intimacy, mostly imagined.

This pet-naming, as far as I can tell, is not

done by women. Not in my experience.

Before the closure of the last pit some of the men moved from pit to pit, as one by one they closed. Refusing the Judas money that bought their jobs they kept working underground to the last. My Joe was one of these. He had an uncle and two grandfathers killed underground, but he loved it, see? Loved the veins of the earth.

One day I put his dinner in front of him and looked absently at his curls hoping there'd be enough for him. The only thing we quarrel about is food. He has the appetite of a wolf. There is no filling him. Sometimes if his plate seems short he erupts like a great volcano. In my mother's generation I might have got a clout for it, but things are different nowadays. I'm no battered wife.

'Few of us transferring down to Maryfield,' he said through a mouth of potato. 'That is, if we want to go.' He munched away. As usual he talked without looking at me. He wiped his mouth with the back of his hand. 'You'll remember Maryfield?'

My fork stayed poised. Maryfield. There was this accident. In the end they just walled up the seam. Never got near the men.

Joes eyes were on me now. Cool. Grey.

I shivered.

'All that stuff makes no difference,' he said, reading my thoughts. 'There's good coal down at Maryfield. Deep seams. And it's on no closing list.' He put his knife and fork together and sat back, forcing his chair on its back legs. I've lost two chairs that way.

'As far as you know, it's not on any list,' I said, biting my lips on pleas for him to come above ground with the rest of us, to take the judas money and try for a job in one of the factories. I had tried pleading before and he had laughed in my face, telling me to mind my own business.

After tea he kicked a ball about a bit with our Patrick and Sean then sat down and read the newspaper—every word, every article for sale, every house for sale, every birth, every marriage, every death. Then went down his allotment to feed his livestock, just like his dad before him and his dad before that.

You can tell Joe was an old-fashioned kind of lad. He'd never even been to a disco. His world was the pit and the garden. He never called it an allotment. Just the garden. My friends thought I was crazy, getting on with a lad who had never even been to a dance. I liked that, then. Thought he was steady and reliable. After my own shiftless father these were good things. And Joe was big and really good looking then, even with pit dust in his golden curls.

Except for a Saturday night he wasn't even interested in going to the pub. Always the garden. He spent such a long time down there. The fresh air and the animals were a good change from the pit. And from me.

Joe's move to Maryfield pit didn't make much of a change at first. He had to set out to work earlier, got back later, He was even hungrier and my supermarket bills went up again. He sold a couple of pigs and bought a breeding sow. Breeding! I did tell him he needn't bring any runts down to my hearth. I like my house nice and he knows that.

When he's been to the pub with his friend Theo on Saturday night, Joe and me do our usual thing. He doesn't push himself on you but he does like the usual thing on a Saturday night. Nothing fancy, mind. You see strange antics in the films nowadays. Even on the telly. They make such a meal of it don't they? Me, I think it's far-fetched. I couldn't be bothered. There was one time Joe said turn over and let's try it that way. I said no fear. This way was bad enough. So he didn't bother.

Joe's *marrer*, Theo, shares the allotment with him. They've been friends since they were born. Their mothers had been friends. Joe and Theo worked *marrers* at the pit before Theo saw the light and got a job in a factory.

Occasionally Theo came to the house. Usually when he was here, neither of them would say much, just watch telly with a word for each other now and then. But there were times when they would hammer away at each other battling for victory in much repeated arguments. It might be the closure, pigs, the council, or the bloody prime minister. They did go on.

They had this do about a breeding sow. It was pigging but there was a bit of bother. The two of them clucked away about it and in the end they decided to sit with her in shifts so the poor dear wouldn't feel too lonely. There was something really motherly about the way those two took care of their stock. Like little lasses playing with their dolls. Mind you my Joe was never motherly with our Patrick and Sean. I didn't see him for dust when I was having them.

Well, the sow survived and there were ten more hungry squealing mouths to feed down at the garden. So Joe went before work to feed them. One night he came home very late after feeding the pigs. 'What happened?' I asked.

'Theo didn't turn up. That's what happened,' he growled. 'And the sow's rolled on two of her young'ns.' He looked down at his dinner, dry and shrunken on the plate, and pushed it away. 'I cannot eat that.'

I pushed it back towards him. 'Not my fault you were late, Joe. Blame Theo.'

He threw the plate in my direction. I could feel the breeze as it passed my ear. The children cried and I swept them up to bed, and went to bed myself. I lay there listening to Joe banging and crashing in the kitchen.

You wouldn't believe the mess that greeted me the next morning. Joe gone. No fire. Bread spilling out of its wrapper, beans spilling out of upturned tins. Burnt toast on the surface unit.

That winter, Joe's journey to work through the icy dark became more treacherous. I watched the weather on the telly and through the window, imagining his struggling with his mates to get our old car away. I even started to scan the jobs page in the paper to find something he might fancy close by. But I knew I would never get him away from the pit, not until the pit went away from under him.

All over the country the pits were finally closing and I was glad. Joe would have to come up into the surface world in the end. Whatever happens the last thing I want for my boys is life in the pit: a life that sucks you away from your family and only leaves you available for your *marrers*.

One night when the snow was still lying in a slushy crust at the edge of the pavements Joe actually came home on time. I'd made a good dinner: leek puddings and steak and kidney with that touch of garlic that even Joe liked these days. The boys had gulped down their dinners and were upstairs on their computer, an early Christmas present, thanks to the lucrative pigs.

Joe ate three mouthfuls and pushed his plate away, folding his lips tight together.

'What's the matter with it?' My voice was really sharp.

He stared down at his plate. 'The dinner?

Nothing. Looks okay. But I'm not that hungry.'

'Are you feeling bad or something?'

'No. I'm fine. I tell you I'm fine.'

I stared at him over my tea cup. He looked all right. A bit red and weather-beaten but he was always like that.

He got up from the table and went upstairs to talk to the lads. Later he even saw them to bed and tucked them in. I could hear his deep voice, talking away with them. I couldn't remember when he'd done that. Ever.

When he came back down I had everything neat and tidy. I got out my cross-stitch and sat in the chair by the fire. He lay down on the couch and closed his eyes.

'You're not going down the garden, Joe?' I said.

'Theo said he'd feed the pigs tonight. He's dropping over here, after.' He spoke without opening his eyes.

I leaned across and turned on the television.

Theo arrived ten minutes later. He's even taller than Joe. Heavier too. He smiles when he talks to you and looks you in the eye. He laughs at your jokes. When he's in the house the air is lighter, the laughter easier. Women really like Theo but nobody's managed to snaffle him yet. Joe says he's too light on his feet to get caught. Even our kids like Theo and they're both a bit reserved and cautious like their dad.

Tonight he cocked his head at the sleeping

Joe. 'That idle sod been sleeping long?'

'Twenty minutes, maybe. Something's up with him. Wouldn't eat his tea and that's not like him.'

Theo grimaced. 'I thought summat was up when he called and asked me to feed.'

As I made him some tea in the kitchen I thought how different they were, him and Joe.

I could hear voices so I put out an extra pot. When I took the tray in Joe was sitting up, quite relaxed. Theo reported back on the animals and went on to describe a fist fight he had got into at work, with the time and motion man.

They murmured away and my cross-stitch needle went in and out, in and out. Then my ears hooked onto what Joe was actually saying. '... along downbye, on me own to do me check ... pitch black it was. No light but me own, like a moth's light in the black. You know what it's like, *marrer*. That black.'

Theo nodded. 'I hated it, that black. Drove me off in the end.'

'Well, I must of lost my bearings cause I turned on this curve and I came to a blank wall. I knew straight off it was where they walled up after the bang. Can't say it bothered me.' He leaned towards Theo, his cup held loosely in his hand. 'But this thing... I turned a corner just about there and there looking down at me from this wall was this giant pitman, taller than any man, I'm tellen yer.'

Theo frowned and I held my breath.

'Me bloody heart!' said Joe. 'It musta jumped straight onto me ribs. This giant is there by the wall, glittering, shining out at me. I turn off my lamp. He vanishes. Not a sound. Not a breath. Then I turn it on again and there he is, larger than life. This bloody giant of a man.'

'So what was it, *marrer?*' said Theo softly. 'Had to be sommat.'

Joe sniffed. 'Turns out it was this picture of a man, kind of stuck on the wall. Silver paper, chocolate wrappers stuck in crevices, picking out the helmet, the pick-axe, the lamp. Even the fingernails. So when your lamp light flashes, he's there.'

'Bloody silly joke, that,' grunted Theo.

'I don't know,' I found myself speaking aloud. 'Maybe it was some kind of memorial, you know? To the men that died?'

Both men turned then, to look at me with cold curiosity, as though I'd just landed from Venus.

Joe coughed, his cheeks flaring. 'Maybe. You never know.' His tone was indifferent, dismissive. He turned his face away from me towards Theo. 'Like I said, *marrer,* me heart was fit to bust.'

I bent over my sewing, tucking my chin close to my chest. As the two of them talked on tears splodged onto my thread, making it impossible to work. When I allowed myself

103

to listen to them again they had changed the subject, talking now about the availability of jobs at Theo's factory and the possibility of Joe working there.

In the end Joe waited until, in its turn, Maryfield Pit was closed. I offered to move away with him to this pit in the Midlands that was still working. He wouldn't hear of that. He did not say as much but I knew he would not work away from his garden, from his pigs, or from his *marrer*.

He's happy enough now working at the factory alongside Theo. They have acquired this second allotment and keep hens as well as pigs. Our sons are at the comprehensive now, where they compete with their mates for everything and comradeship is thing of the past. I have a part time job working for a mail order firm and am taking exams in English and Biology at college. Sometimes I am not in to make Joe's tea but he doesn't comment.

And at last there are no pits any more: no ghosts of the past, in the flesh or tricked out in silver paper on a wall of coal. I have to say it quietly round here but I think that's a very a good thing.

9 Oh, Amsterdam

When Ernestine's husband Peter died she mourned him sadly but underneath the sadness she was instantly aware of these bubbles of possibility. There was the possibility of never again having to cook on a gas barbecue in some chilly god-forsaken campsite by a loch or halfway up a mountain. Never again would she have to walk twenty-mile bridleways or coast-to-coast paths to prove she could do it. Never again would she have check some building for an eighteenth century pediment or a medieval roof line.

Although she never cried for months after his death she still thought about him. She was never really alone. She could still hear echoes of his voice, telling her to watch her step, look here, look there, to see this interesting thing, or that disgraceful outfit.

Throughout her twenty-year marriage Ernestine had watched with clinical interest as her friends and colleagues went on their holidays to the exciting parts of the world that she herself would have loved to visit. For her camping was more work than travel. Four months after John's death when she was finally used to running her own bank account, it occurred to her that travel was a real possibility. So she filled in her passport form and began to work out in principle her own particular notion of travel.

This idea began to crystallise in lunchtime discussions with her friend Marian who had worked in the office with her at Juggerland Plumbing Wholesalers since they started as sixteen year olds. Marian and her sister Bet were great travellers. They had even seen the Great Wall of China. But, as Ernestine listened to Marian's tales Ernestine realised that Marian liked to hobble herself with all kinds of preconceptions about the place she was about to visit. Before visiting a place she would read dozens of books to tell her what to think and what to see about a place, and after she had been there, she would read them again to find out what she had thought and had seen. Ernestine privately wondered whether Marian might just as well not have gone to these places. The books were surely enough.

This was not, decided Ernestine, her idea of travel.

As the months went on she became aware that she herself had been party to this very kind of hobbling in her life with Peter. She reflected on all those nights when Peter would spread maps on the dining table and plan their walks the next day to the last step. She remembered her frustration at Peter's laughter when she complained that they might miss something, something unexpected on their journey. 'Just tell me what you want to see, honey, and I will build it into the master plan.' One time (in her head) Ernestine retorted that all she ever saw was the muddy heels of Peter's boots as he strode on in front of her. But of course he never heard those words as she never spoke them out loud.

Five months after Peter's death his voice only rang occasionally in Ernestine's ears and she began to feel that in the end, she would be able to go to all the places she had dreamed of. The money was not yet sorted but she was anxious to start on her adventure even though she realised that she had to crawl before she could walk. Then, while sorting Peter's books in the back room she came across her own school copy of *The Diary of Anne Frank*.

Oh, Amsterdam! Yes. Amsterdam make a good start. A short journey. A couple of nights stay. Her first, her very own experiment in travel.

She rejected a mountain of unasked-for information from Marian about books she should read, places to see and places to avoid, in this dangerous city. No, she said to Marian, she wouldn't be visiting either the Rijksmuseum or the Van Gogh Museum. And no, she didn't need accommodation brochures as she was sure she could find a place to stay when she arrived. Marian was aghast at the idea.

As she had a farewell drink with Marian at their favourite watering hole, the Grange

Hotel in Market Street, her friend asked her whether perhaps it was too early. 'Peter's just been ... well, not here for five months. You are still in shock Ernestine. You've not adjusted. This crazy journey's ill conceived. I'm telling you. You should have someone with you.'

'The whole point is that I have to go on my own.' Ernestine put her hand on her friend's arm. 'It's time, Marian. If I don't do it now I'll end up camping in the Cairngorms on automatic pilot with a group of lost souls. That'll be the beginning of the end, be sure of that.'

Marian shook her head. 'Talk about innocents abroad! You take the biscuit, Ernestine.'

*   *   *

At Schiphol Airport Ernestine made it easily through customs and collected her modest luggage. She bought fifty pounds worth of currency at the Bureau de Change and put it in the special purse she had brought for that purpose. On a flashing notice near the concourse she found a free telephone number by a picture of a bed and rang and booked a cheap city centre hotel, sight unseen. Even across the North Sea she could hear Marian's indrawn breath: for her, cheap hotels were the lairs of Satan.

Standing in line for the bus she felt a kind of tingling that started at her heels and swept up through her body. She had done it. She smiled. Now it was starting. The bus from the airport went to the city centre and unloaded its passengers who gathered their luggage and set off purposefully about the next stage of their journey. Ernestine looked at the piece of paper in her hand. Just an address. She would need a map. A taxi. A taxi would do the trick. She found a taxi queue and joined it. When her turn came the driver, longfaced with sharp bird-like eyes with an enquiring look, looked disappointed when she showed him her piece of paper. The hotel must be very nearby. He looked past her. 'Anyone for Schiphol?' He shouted in vain at the taxi queue, before proceeding to take her the very longest way round to her hotel which, she later discovered, was three minute's walk from the taxi-rank.

Her hotel was a wonderfully tall, extremely narrow house in Rokin Street off the central Damplatz. In the tiny reception that doubled as a bar, the concierge, a thin young man in his thirties, smiled politely at her. In near-flawless English he informed her that sadly there was no lift. He didn't offer to carry her luggage. As she tramped up the fourth flight of the picturesque staircase she realised that the hotel was cheap was not because it was a brothel or a drug centre as Marian thought. It was just a clean, faintly elegant, six storeyed, one room wide dog-kennel catering for people passing through this busy city.

Her room was on the very top floor. She had to duck to get across her garret room to unpack and hang up her clothes, before changing into the new green linen trouser suit she had bought especially for Amsterdam. Then she sat down at the narrow window and looked down into the street below feeling like a goddess viewing the comings and goings of the mere mortals down there: men, women, children, shoppers, tourists, cars and bicycles, trams lumbering up and down on their central reservation. There must have been some rain, because the road and the pavements were wet, gleaming in the soft afternoon light.

She smiled. She very nearly laughed out loud. She had really done it! She had come here on her own, found a hotel, and settled in. It was easy. You didn't need to travel with someone you didn't particularly like, or go to places where there were only people like you. You could travel on your own and be on your own. You could be a stranger and see what only a stranger could see, unfiltered by other people's ideas and preconceptions.

Still smiling she picked up her handbag and made her way down the six flights of stairs and out into the city streets. Her nose prickled with the warm over-rich smell that hit her as she walked along the pavement: a combination of wine, food, foetid water and petrol fumes.

Peter's voice whispered in her ear that this was the smell of decay. 'Relish the clean air of the mountains, Ernestine, better than this murk,'

'Oh, shut up Peter!' she muttered. She gulped a whole lungful of the air and told Peter in her head that it was all right. Every place must have its own smell, Peter, and you should welcome it.

The canal grids made the city centre very easy to navigate. After one or two wanders when she found herself back on the same corner, she worked out that she could always find her way back to Rokin Street so that was all right. She had made herself safe.

Alongside one canal she stopped at a bookstall under a neat canopy. The bookseller was sitting on a tall stool on one corner, filing his nails. The books were all English or American with a scattering of French texts. There were two other customers. A short silver haired man in a creased white jacket was turning the pages of what looked like an academic tome. A boy was sitting down on the wet pavement, his head down over a battered paperback.

Ernestine found a very decent copy of *Catch Twenty Two* and was just paying for it when she spotted a copy of *Tender Is The Night*, so she bought that as well, after the merest struggle with the currency in her special purse. The bookseller wrapped them in a brown paper parcel for her with a little loop in the string so they would be easy to carry.

She walked on, turned another corner by the canal and found herself in a very different place. She thought of Marian. Here it was as though the lights had flickered and come on a little brighter. With her sharp peripheral vision Ernestine caught sight of women lounging in what would have been shop windows. Clearly the women themselves were the goods on offer. She saw all shapes and sizes of women in various states of undress. She felt herself blushing, put her head down and started to hurry, Peter's voice in her ear saying 'How could you do this Ernestine, you foolish woman?'

'Oh will you shut up!' she muttered out loud. 'Shut up!'

'Can I help you?'

She swung round to see who was talking to her. It was the man from the bookstall, the one in the crumpled white suit. 'What did you say?' she said. 'Did you speak to me?'

'I wondered if I could help. You seemed a bit distressed back there.' He nodded along the canal to the windows with the posturing woman.

'No, no. It was just... Well, to be honest I turned the corner and there they were. Those women.'

He laughed. 'Very full on, as they say. The Dutch are very honest about some things.' He put out his hand. 'I'm John Lulworth, here to see the sights.' He talked with this strange American accent, crisp rather than drawling.

She shook hands with him. 'Ernestine Smith. I'm here as well to see the sights. It's the first time I've been in Amsterdam.'

'It sure is an interesting place.'

They stood there on the corner in silence with people flowing round them like water splitting round a stone in a stream. Then he moved so he was beside her, took her arm and guided her onto a bridge over the canal. He leaned on the balustrade and she followed suit. Below them the gleaming brown water moved like shaken silk, reflecting the trees and narrow houses on the opposite bank. She leaned, making way through the water. She tensed up, suddenly too aware of the man beside her.

'I noticed you have a taste for Scott Fitzgerald,' he said finally.

She breathed out. 'So I do. I have read *The Great Gatsby* five times. He is so easy to read, I think, but subtle. My husband used to tell me it was a waste of time to read a book more than once. But every time I read it there was something more to see, or feel.'

'Guy's some writer. Not everyone gets him. But he's some writer.' He looked along the pavement in both directions. 'Is he here? Your husband?'

'Not any more. He died. Five, six months ago.'

'I'm sorry. I should not have...'

She interrupted him. 'You don't have to be sorry. It was not your fault. I am getting used to it. That's what I was doing when you stopped me. Talking to him. Or answering him. It's hard to get out of the habit.'

He stared at her. 'Look! Can I buy you a coffee? I know a place. Real old Amsterdam!'

She only considered for a moment, then nodded. In for a penny, in for a pound. All part of the adventure, after all. She could just imagine Marian's face. 'You picked up a man? In the brothel district?'

The man led the way down a side street and through a narrow doorway into a small room packed with tables. It was painted a dirty yellow and the customers, definitely not tourists, watched closely as he found a table and pulled back a chair for her. It must have been like that going back centuries: through two wars and goodness knows what else.

The other customers were all men, some in work overalls and caps. All dour, even malevolent. Now it was Marian whispering in her ear, this time about the white slave-trade. The man behind the counter, small with a black apron nodded at her companion. 'Coffee?' he said.

John Lulworth looked at her and she nodded. 'Two coffees,' he said.

As they drank their small cups of black bitter coffee, he smiled at her. 'I really like the colour of your suit. Mint green, My favourite colour. I noticed it at the bookstall.'

Ernestine smoothed the creased sleeve of her suit but could not think of what to say.

After that, between sips of coffee John Lulworth told her things about himself. He was some kind of consultant. He seemed to know Amsterdam quite well and had given himself a day in the city on his way to a medical conference in Maastricht. 'That's also a very old city. Do you know Maastricht?'

She shook her head. 'Can I ask you something?'

'Anything.'

'Why did you stop and talk to me?'

'What can I say? You looked like a nice person. I liked your green suit. I liked your choice of books. Then I saw you in the street talking to yourself and I thought you might need company.' He ducked his silver head back over his coffee.

She looked at him reflectively. He was rumpled, older than her by perhaps fifteen years. Quite old, then. It didn't really seem like a pick-up, no matter what Marian might have said. Even so, he had still followed her from the book-stall.

Her glance wandered away from him and round the café. It was very old. It must have been the same in those days, when Anne Frank was alive, before they bundled her and her family into the lorry. In the long years before the occupation, Anne's father and her uncles might even have come here to this café, drunk this same bitter coffee and argued about trade or books: free and alive without really knowing it. Of course that was another Amsterdam in another universe, before the culture-vultures, the invasion of the thrill-seekers, the drug-users, and the people who stopped over on their way to conferences.

But some things don't change. Anne's father and uncles would still acknowledge this present Amsterdam, would recognise the same fine buildings as they crushed together, preening themselves in their reflections in the canals. They would know this café. She felt sure of it.

Ernestine stood up. 'I'll have to go.'

'Do you?' He looked at his watch. 'You have an appointment?'

'Yes.' Mentally she thanked him for supplying the lie. 'I am meeting a friend.'

'Ah. I had hoped we might dine,' he said. 'That's a pity.'

'It is,' she agreed. 'A pity.'

He signalled the waiter and paid the bill. Outside the café they shook hands and she walked quickly along the alleyway back to the canal. She glanced round once but there was no sign of him. She found her way back to hotel in Rokin Street very easily. Well done, Ernestine, she thought.

She sat down in the tiny bar and the young

concierge poured her a gin and tonic. This was a new taste for her and she liked it. Glass in hand she looked round. In the table by the tall thin window a couple were sharing a bottle of red wine. The man was middle-aged, the woman was much younger than he was, and they were clearly not married. As they talked the girl leaned over to touch the man's arm and the bangles on her arm rattled.

Then without warning, and to her own mortification, tears began to fall in torrents down Ernestine's cheeks. The young woman reached down into her gilt clasp bag and handed her a wad of tissues. The concierge poured her another gin, but the tears still kept flowing. She tried to smile through her tears. In the end they were all laughing at Ernestine's helpless state and she had to escape, still crying, to climb the eight flights of stairs to her room. In there she stripped off and stood under the tiny shower until the water was tepid and the tears finally stopped.

Then, shivering she patted herself down with the large towel, tied it round herself and made her way across the tiny room to the window. She must have been a long time crying and showering because now she could see the town in its mantle of night, glittering and glowing like a turning diamond, steep roofs scratching against the sky, windows twinkling with the interior life. The distant gleam of black water.

The American was out there, dining somewhere. Perhaps she should have gone with him. He was a nice man. There would have been no harm eating with him. She shook her head. Far too soon. Most of all, on this the first of her journeys, she wanted to be on her own.

A tram rattling past, its bright windows spotlighting a scattering of passengers, brought her eye back to the glittering night. Of course the night would not have been so glittering when Anne Frank looked out on it from her hidden attic. The darkness of wartime streets; the dingy threat of the engines of unseen trucks. Ernestine leaned further out of the window, wondering just where in this city Anne Frank lived. Which house, which street was first her refuge, then the place of her betrayal? Marian whispered in her ear that Ernestine should have read the guide book.

She glanced down at the street to see a woman looking up at her, as she sat half-naked in her narrow window. She pulled back quickly and as she did so she disturbed a pile of leaflets on the windowsill. *The Rijksmuseum. The Van Gogh Museum. Anne Frank's House.*

Then Peter's voice was in her ear. 'Take a look, Ernestine. For Christ's sake, take a look!'

She pulled on her nightdress, climbed onto the bed and laid out the leaflets on the bedspread. Which one first? She had the whole day tomorrow. Perhaps she should go and see them all. It would all be very interesting: something to talk to Marian about, when she got home.

Then she would plan her next journey. Perhaps Prague. That had a nice ring to it. Prague.

10 Knives

Ronald Parfitt had worked as a typing pool secretary for fourteen years and, as he repeatedly told his dear mother, he was well suited to it. Even liked it. At first the other secretaries, all women, had whispered in his presence and been slow in their response to his meandering queries about layout and copies.

Within seven years in the typing pool Ronald became the person that newcomers would ask about layout and copies. He answered queries quickly and precisely, with, as he told his mother, more consideration than he had enjoyed in the early days.

After that first month's hassle Ronald had no worries. The work did not infringe on his precious spare time. Most importantly it did not impede the progress of the armies marching in still splendour across the floor of the spare bedroom of his mother's semi in Willesdon.

His mother Mrs Parfitt would often chuckle with her buddies from aerobics about her Ronald playing with his soldiers. At least it kept Ronald out of mischief. You knew what boys were, these days.

Ronald—at 44, with thinning hair and a neatly rounded belly nurtured by his mother's home cooking and his nightly two cans of

120

Guinness—was hardly a *boy*. But his mother and he liked to play this game.

The consumption of Guinness was another game—an open secret between them. It was never consumed in his mother's presence. She had made him aware almost from the cradle that her hatred of alcohol had precipitated the early and swift exit of her husband, Ronald's father 41 years ago, into the arms of a more tolerant barmaid from Fulham.

Ronald consumed the Guinness upstairs in the spare bedroom while he fought the Battle of Borodino or the Battle of Waterloo. The drink added savour to his personal victories which were often pulled off in the role of an Irish mercenary in the French army. The Irishman frequently performed amazing routs which turned the decision of the battle to the admiration—sometimes the consternation—of the generals on both sides.

One drawback to his life was that Ronald had never had a serious girlfriend, nor had he experienced directly the joys of consummation of the deepest affections of a man and a woman. However, in order to ensure that he would never be wrong-footed by this lack of experience, he obtained books and pictures that allowed him to study the matter of consummation of relationships at a safe distance, in vivid colour and detail. He kept this material under his bed. Their presence in his life was another open secret between him and his mother.

One day at work a whole shoal of tapes started to come down to the typists in the pool from a new man, Mr Gargett. This new man generated such a great deal of work that the firm had to employ a new girl to help to spread the load.

At first Ronald took very little notice of the new girl. Marylin was quiet, kept her head down at her terminal. Then after a few days he began to notice her mole-coloured hair and her clothes that were of an indeterminate grey or brown. She wore loose jackets that robbed her shape of definition.

Looking at her more closely Ronald noticed that she had very white legs and fragile ankles, fine and bird-like. Sometimes he raised his head from his screen to watch her ankles as they walked the full length of the office. Watching her walk became part of the pleasures of his day

Most of the girls went out at lunchtime to have a sandwich in the Mall and perhaps to shop for their husbands' dinners that night. Ronald had his lunch in the canteen. As he bent down over his pizza Ronald sometimes daydreamed about his colleagues and those dinners and the domestic cosiness that might succeed them, and the bedtime frolics that might succeed that. He had resigned himself to the fact that this was not his lot. Even so he did relish the daydreams. They were very pleasant, those daydreams.

But things were changing. Marylin did not go to the mall. She stayed at her station, two behind his, and opened a plastic box containing a jumble of tomatoes, cheese and cold potato. As she munched these she held her plastic fork close to her cheek, raising her little finger daintily in the air. After she had had her lunch she would take out a magazine or book and read in silence until the polite whine of the buzzer instructed her to log on again.

One day Ronald, returning from the lavatory, glanced over her shoulder and realised she was reading a highly coloured magazine that devoted itself to weapons and militaria. A shock travelled through him from the nape of his neck through the pit of his stomach to his toes. He knew the magazine very well. He had its twin on his bedside table, on top of other editions going back two years.

As he took up Mr Gargett's tape and set it in his transcribing machine, Ronald's blood was zooming. His heart was pounding. His brain boomeranged. His fingers raced at lightning speed over his keyboard transforming Mr Gargett's spit-bullet words into reasonable syntax and more or less graceful prose.

As he typed he pictured himself with Marylin, the pair of them poring over his battle scenes with her making very useful strategic suggestions. He saw the two of them eating

123

toast before the gas fire in the spare bedroom. He saw her lying back on the narrow bed in a pose lifted from one of his private pictures. He blinked hard then and tried to imagine a body of flesh and blood under those floating blues and browns, above those fragile ankles.

In the next few days Marylin was on his mind all the time. He waited for her to arrive, watched her as she worked and ate her lunch. But still he could not quite bring himself to speak to her directly. In the evenings he began to drink more Guinness so his gurgling stomach kept him awake, causing him to prowl the distance between his bedroom and the lavatory several times. And to his mother's annoyance he did not eat his usual egg and bacon breakfasts.

One day he had an inspiration. He would wear the waistcoat he kept especially for his monthly visits to his Wargame Club in Enfield. As he walked past her he was aware that Marylin took a satisfying second look at the waistcoat, which was nicely figured in an abstract design of tiny scimitars formed into stars. That day Marylin held his gaze as he returned from lunch. Her eyes were glittering black, like glistening tarmac shining after recent rain. 'Rotten weather,' she said, smiling slightly.

'Lousy,' he muttered, scuttling past. Then he looked back in her direction. 'Settled down here, have you?' At last he had done it. He had spoken to her.

She shrugged. 'Much as you would anywhere.'

He took a breath. 'So, where were you before, then? Where did you work?'

'Offices, mostly. I did do a bit of nursing.'

'Nursing?' His heart leapt at the thought of her in uniform, the ragged mole-coloured hair caught back in a white veil. 'At least that's a profession you can do a bit of good.'

'It was all right.' She smiled that slight smile of hers and put on her earphones. His heart sang. 'Long hours, though,' she said. 'And people aren't always grateful, you know.'

He put on his own earphones. 'I don't suppose that can happen. People can be funny. I know that myself.'

As he typed away he gave himself a mental pat on the back. Didn't do so bad, Ron. A little bit of chit-chat about this and that. No rocket science. He felt taller, more manly somehow now. He had breached the citadel.

That night after work he followed Marylin down the stairs, enjoying the sight of her twinkling white ankles under her long grey coat. Later, as he passed her at the bus stop in his immaculate car, her head jerked up, and he knew something had happened between them. He had not imagined it. His life was on the cusp of change. He knew it.

At home that night he pushed his plate away without touching his dinner. His mother threw down her sports bag, sat down and folded her arms. 'Ronald Parfitt, you eat your dinner or I'll not go to my aerobics. I'm telling you, I'm not moving from here till you've eaten your dinner.'

He glared at her. Once when he was six she put on his coat and dragged him halfway along the road, saying that, seeing as he refused to eat his dinner she was taking him to the council and putting him into care. She had only relented when, on bended knees, he had begged her to please take him home and he would eat his dinners for ever and ever. And ever.

Now, he pulled his plate towards him and sampled a forkful of potato. She smiled and stood up. 'There, Ronnie. You know it's not good for you to miss your meals.' She ruffled his thin hair as she passed. He waited till he heard the door click behind her and threw his knife to the floor with a clatter. 'Bitch,' he said. 'Stupid bitch.'

The next lunchtime as he set out for lunch Marylin looked up at him and smiled. 'All right?' she said.

'All right,' he nodded.

She pulled her close collar away from her neck. 'How does this heat suit you?'

'Quite well, actually.' His voice squeaked perilously in his ears. 'Can't do with the cold.'

'Ronald...' she paused.

He held his breath.

'… I hope you don't mind me asking you…'

He laughed heartily then, achieving just the right tone of hearty reassurance. 'Ask away, Marylin. Ask away.'

'I saw you in your car last night. You have a car.'

'So I have. Riley Elf. Really rare. Collector's item, actually. I've been offered thousands for it.'

'I bet.'

'So?' he cleared his throat.

'Well, this is the thing Ronald. I'm having difficulties with my flatmates. The girls I share with. The place is teeming. All these visitors. In and out, in and out. No consideration.'

'People can be funny,' he said cautiously. 'I know that.' He wasn't going to tell her he still lived with his mum.

'Well, I've seen this flat advertised in the paper. Out at Narrowell.' She saw the look on his face. 'I know, I know! It's a grotty area. But it's cheap. You know the wage we get here.'

'Don't I!'

'Well, it's like this.' She spread out her fingers and surveyed her hands. Ronald thought her hands were beautiful. Like delicate starfish. She went on. 'I have this appointment to see this flat in Narrowell after work. But it's very difficult, a woman on her own. You know. You read things.'

He nodded. He'd read some of those reports very carefully himself. There were

127

versions of such episodes in the stash under his bed. Blacker versions of course.

'Well, Ronald, I was wondering if you'd be kind enough to take me there. Keep an eye, out sort of thing. It's empty. I have the key.'

He glanced around the office, his heart singing. She asked him. He didn't have to make the move.

She sensed his hesitation. 'I'll wait for you on the bus stop, Ronald. No one here need know.'

He breathed out. 'No problem, then. No problem at all. I'll take you there after work.'

Five minutes before the end of the day he went to the washroom and washed his face and neck, hands and wrists. He scrambled under his shirt to apply some new roll-on deodorant, bought on his way back from lunch from Mr Patel on the corner. As he went to his desk he didn't look at Marylin.

Ten minutes later he caught sight of her standing at the bus stop in her long grey coat and stopped. She got into the car her coat sagging open as she reached for the handle. As she did so Ronald caught a glimpse of something that made his heart pound. Nestling in the lining of her coat, neatly stitched into webbing holsters were three sharp kitchen knives in graded sizes.

'Well,' she said brightly, smiling at him. 'Shall we go Ronald?'

As he steered his car through meaner and

meaner streets, down narrower and narrower alleyways, Ronald's body was humming with terror. He flinched when Marylin put her narrow hand on his sleeve to indicate they were there.

'Here. The blue door I think.' She laughed vivaciously, showing small pearly teeth. He eased on the brake and she climbed out. She leaned in towards the window and he had another glimpse of the knives. 'Won't you come in with me?' she said, her black eyes shining wetly in the late sun. 'It would be a help to have a man's perspective on the flat.'

'No. No,' he mumbled. 'I'll keep watch here.' He sat there sweating until the peeling scratched door of the house closed behind her. And then, very quietly he set the car in gear and allowed it to ease away, gathering speed as it charged through Narrowell, losing speed as he neared home.

His mother was surprised to see him. 'I thought it was a club night, for your playing soldiers.' she grumbled. 'I haven't even got your dinner on. You'll just have to sort for yourself.' She slammed the door behind her as she went.

He had beans on toast and was in bed when she got home. The next morning he was violently sick and his mother had to call the doctor. In the days following he ate nothing and drank only boiled water. When he felt slightly better he spent some fruitful hours in the spare bedroom cataloguing his soldier collection, before putting it to rest in its storage boxes. The only soldier he kept out was the Irish mercenary, his favourite, his alter ego, that he placed on his bedside table beside his clock, his night glass and his Art Deco lamp.

It was three weeks before he finally crept back to work and although he knew she knew he was there, not once did he glance in Marylin's direction. At lunchtime he went out to the canteen in the opposite direction. She walked past his station several times. He could feel her beside him like a shadow over water but still he refused to look at her. After a week, much to his relief, she gave up bothering about him at all.

One day he was transcribing one of Mr Gargett's tapes when he realised he was typing Marylin's name. He wound back the tape and listened again. It was a testimonial, a reference for a job. *'Miss Holroyd is quiet, trustworthy, an assiduous worker ... a return to nursing is appropriate for her attributes...'*

At the end of that week Marylin vanished from her station, to be replaced by a zippy young mum, keen to return to work. Safe. Now Ronald felt safe.

Now he began to regain his appetite and eat everything his mother put before him. He put his scimitar waistcoat and the boxed soldiers up into the loft and joined the Riley

Elf Owners Guild, which had some very interesting meetings. And a whole crowd of very nice people who knew Riley Elfs from nose to tip and inside out.

It was just before the Christmas break, three months later that Ronald saw the article. He had just finished a double helping of the inevitable Wednesday mince and dumplings and his mother, ready to go to yoga in her pink quilted jacket, was clearing away, clashing the dishes in the sink. Restless at the non-arrival of his Riley Elf magazine, Ronald picked up the newspaper that she had left, folded neatly, by his plate.

He spread it before him, aligning it carefully with the edge of the cleared table. He glanced at page one and then turned straight to page two. He looked, blinked hard then looked again. The top half of the page was an article about a young woman who had just been committed to a secure hospital in the West Country. Apparently she had murdered an old person who was in her care. She had stabbed him seven times in some kind of frenzy. There would be no proper trial as the woman was declared unfit to plead.

And there, beside the report, staring back at him in grainy black and white and looking demure under her thatch of pulled-back hair, was Marylin. Beside her was a policewoman. He shuddered.

His mother, hoisting her black sateen

131

rucksack onto her back looked at him sharply. 'What is it Ronald?' she said. 'Are you all right?'

Ronald shuffled the paper and lined up the page headed Articles For Sale. 'Nothing, mother,' he said. 'Nothing at all. I'm quite all right. Now.'

His mother stared at him thoughtfully. 'So what will you do tonight, then?'

'Dunno. Maybe I'll get my soldiers down from the loft and set them up. Maybe I'll fight the battle of Borodino.'

She smiled faintly. 'That's right. You enjoy yourself son. I'm late. I've gotta go. Be late for my class.'

11 Glass

The Woman

Bettina sat very still, listening closely to the alien noise somewhere above her, on the roof. Then she heard another, more muffled, rolling, persistent sound. She closed her eyes and in her sharp mind's eye could see this soft, padded body rolling from the spine of the roof. Then it stopped, lodged, she surmised, against one of the big vicarage chimneys.

Her hand went towards the telephone then pulled away. Thomas would not *exactly* say she was an over-imaginative fool, but his voice would be drenched in its usual purring kindness, its characteristic moderation. Telephoning Thomas was always a velvet-lined dead end. She knew her husband lived in fear of her dark feelings and would rather drown in his own good works with the despairing. Than come home to find himself obliged to thresh about in his wife's despair.

Phoning her doctor would be another kind of dead end. *He* would come running all right! He'd smile and fill her full of pills, make her sleep for two days and forget everything. Including her name. And Orlando's name. And the name of the Chancellor of the Exchequer. Then they'd get out their clipboards and whisk her off to Cherry Knowle, just like the other time.

She made her way past the mountain of black plastic charity sacks cluttering the hall, through to the kitchen where she cleared a small space in the clutter on the kitchen table so she could settle down there with her cup of tea. From here she could hear more clearly the man overhead. She looked up to see a shadow looming across the glass roof. She could hear the scrunch and scrape of shoes on the flat roof alongside it.

She took a deep breath, reached up to the top shelf of the dresser and took down her wonderful glass egg, her comforter. She rolled it between her hands to warm it then held it up to catch the light from the skylight. The white spiral embedded within her egg started to shimmer; she could feel it pulsing against her palm as it started to warm up.

The egg had been a present from Orlando's godmother, Denise, who always bought gifts made in Sunderland. Glass had been made there for a thousand years and local support was Denise's watchword. Thomas, of course, admired Denise for her acumen. Despite all this, this glass egg was Bettina's favourite thing. It had certainly helped her to survive with its comforting ways. Now, warmed by her hand, it started to buzz and hum. Then her body began to vibrate in tune with the egg and a bubble of light started in her solar plexus and started to radiate outwards. She felt warm and very light. Floating.

The floating feeling gave her the courage to look upwards and through the glass she could see the shadowy outline more clearly now. She held the egg up towards the shadow: a temple offering. As though in response the air was suddenly rent with a great cracking sound. A body, bundled in a hooded parka, hurtled down in an eruption of glass, wood and dust, and dropped fair and square on the kitchen table. A boy lay there, very still, measuring his length on the six foot table. Shards of glass sat in the folds of his thick parka and a gash on his cheek was dripping blood. He was young—fifteen perhaps—and his sandy hair tumbled about his shoulders like the rays of the sun. His eyes were closed and he was out to the world.

Bettina reached out and eased his fingers away from the heavy screwdriver that he still clasped in his hand. Then, putting the egg in her mouth for safety, she rooted in a cupboard for some bits of old clothesline to tie his hands and his feet to the table legs.

Just as she—an ex-Guide who had always Been Prepared—finished tying her very effective reef knots, the boy's eyes fluttered open. He came to and started struggling against the ropes. His eyes widened with fear as he saw her looming above him, egg in mouth. 'Jesus!' he said.

135

'Jesus?' She removed the egg from her mouth. 'This is just the house to be saying that,' she said. The egg was cool and wet now in her hand. It had stopped vibrating.

'How's that?' he said, visibly relieved that her face, without the bulging egg, looked relatively normal.

'Didn't you see the sign at the front gate? This is a *vicarage!*'

He whistled. 'Front gate? Never came in no front gate. I hitched down here from Gateshead, hopped across the dual carriageway and came through the gardens and in the back. And this is the biggest house in this row. Good pickin's in big houses.' He paused, and when she just kept staring and said nothing he rushed on. 'Me, I like Sunderland. Big houses, middle sized houses, small streets and then the sea, always the sea. It's got this canny buzz about it, has Sunderland. Then the sea! But a vicarage?' His eyes went past her to the high ceiling and its glass window, discoloured with years of cooking. 'Looks like I'm wasting me time here, like. Appearances can be deceptive.' He pulled hard against his bonds. 'No need for these, missis. Never hurt a soul in my life. I'm tellen yer.' He opened his sapphire blue eyes really wide and looked into hers.

'How would I know that?' She rolled the egg in her hand.

'Teck my word for it, missis.'

136

She laughed then. The laugh radiated round her head and suffused her body, making her feel lighter again. She looked down at her egg, which was starting to pulse again.

'What's that then? That thing in your hand?'

'An egg, idiot! Don't you know an egg when you see one?'

'I thought you were incubating it when I saw you with it in your mouth. Don't some animals do that with their young?' His face scrunched inwards in a combined nod-and-wink and lost its built-in beauty. 'You dinnet seem like no vicar's wife to me, missis.'

She laughed again and pushed back her thick unkempt hair. Perhaps she should untie the boy. He hardly seemed dangerous.

'Let's loose, missis,' he said softly.

She nearly did as he said, but instead, she drew up a chair close to the table. 'Perhaps I should tend to that cut first,' she said placidly. 'Don't want you to bleed to death do we?'

'That'd be a start. You got a plaster or something?'

She looked vaguely round the kitchen. 'I'm not sure.'

He lifted up his head and looked round with some difficulty. 'This place is a fucken mess, missis,' he said, glaring at her. She noticed again the blueness of those eyes, the thick fair lashes fanning upwards. 'Doesn't it bother you?'

137

She shrugged. 'There seems so little time. Little time to do things.' She yawned very widely.

'You're on sommat' missis, en't you?' His voice was sharp.

'On something?'

'Drugs, pills, uppers, downers, blues, whites. That kind of thing.'

She shrugged. 'They push them on me.'

'Don't you take them, that's my advice. Never touch'em myself. In some of the places I've been, they push stuff on you, legal and illegal. They all wanter dumb you down, friends and foes alike.'

She stared at him. 'And what are these places where've you been?'

'Homes, then schools with bars and fat lads with janglin' keys ...' He strained to lift his head again so he could look her in the eye. 'Come on, Missis. Undo me hands at least. It's fucken murder tied up like this. My leg's in cramp. Can't yeh see it shivering of its own accord?'

'Did you really never take any of that stuff?' Bettina did occasionally read a paragraph in Thomas's *Telegraph*. Drugs were rife in those places. 'That stuff they pushed on you, legal and illegal?'

A shake of the head. 'Nah. Never. Hard going not to, but.'

She leaned across and undid the offending foot and rubbed his leg absently. 'So how did you end up those places? And more important, why did you rain in on me like manna from Heaven?'

'They tell us it was misspent youth Missis. Early days I bunked off school, went down town, got up to things. Me Mam and Dad had other things on their minds, like. Dad always on the pop. Then Mam went off her lid and they took her away. Me, I did a bit of grafting. Why, man, the fucken things were laid out for yeh in shops, asking to be taken. But then the mate I was grafting with grasses on us, doesn't he? So I end up in Acklington with the bad lads. Then other places.'

'And now you end up here,' she said, primmer than she felt. 'Plunging in on me like this. Why the roof? Why not break a door or window?'

'They don't spot it, missis, if you get in on the roof. Not for days.'

'Well, I spotted it didn't I?'

'And I spotted you. Through the roof.'

'But I heard you first.'

He groaned. 'Don't do it missis! Don't tell on us. Me sister-in-law Carol's already thrown us out and our Dylan's putty in her painted fingers, see? And with no address I get no fucken dole, see?' He flexed his free knee up towards his chest. 'And if you lay us in now, Missis, they'll have us away for a really, really long time. I'm supposed to be good, or else! I just thought a little light grafting'd get us the money for the fare to Edinburgh.'

'Edinburgh?'

'I've a mate there who's promised us a job. He sells kites on the Royal Mile and needs another pair of hands. Makes a mint. Legal work. Now that's a rare thing.'

'Kites...?'

'So, what's your name, missis?' he interrupted.

She was surprised into an answer. 'Bettina,' she said.

'Bettina? Funny old name, that.'

'It's after a fashion model my grandmother liked.'

'Like that Naomi, yeh mean?'

'Well, more old style, really. High heels and New Look.'

'I know that. Retro. The painted sister-in-law has magazines. Retro's right back in now.' He grinned up at her appealingly. 'Now, Bettina. What about the other foot?'

She shook her head. 'I might be retro, dear, but I'm not out of the ark.'

He lay back. The blood on his cheek was congealing. He changed tack. 'If you untie me I'll clear all this mess up for you. It's like a fucken packin' can in this kitchen. I'm very tidy, you know. They teach you that inside.'

She threw the egg from hand to hand and looked round the room. 'It's all too hard, this,' she said. 'I don't even know where to start.'

He nodded, straining his head up from the

table to catch her eye properly. 'Not starting? My Mam was just like that before they carted her away. And me, I was like that I when I was thirteen. I bunked off school and lay around the house all day. Couldn't stop yawning. Then, when I started a bit of graftin' I was all right again. Adrenaline. Didn't feel so bad at all. Not so tired, like.'

'Are you suggesting I try a bit of gentle grafting?'

He raised his head again and laughed at this, his golden hair lifting and settling in the light from the broken window. 'Nah. It worked for me, like. One time. It was her said my trouble was adrenaline. Too intelligent. Not enough to do. The adrenaline kind of goes bad. At least I think that's what she said. She had great legs, that one. Right up to her armpits.'

Bettina put the egg back in her mouth and started to root in a drawer.

His eyes followed her. 'You look fucken weird with that thing in your mouth, Bettina. If you dinnet mind us saying so.'

She took the egg out of her mouth and placed it carefully in a pink egg-cup on the second shelf of the kitchen unit. 'It's a kind of comfort,' she said. She pulled out a drawer, tipped the contents onto the floor and fished a tin of plasters out of the mess. Then she took a baking bowl and filled it with warm water, found an only slightly soiled towel, and set about cleaning the cut on the boy's face.

The boy lay back on the table and relaxed as she dabbed his cheek. 'So, what family d'you have, Bettina?'

'Well, I don't know what counts as family, really. I did have this son, Orlando. He's fifteen. But he's not here now.'

'Orlando? I thought that was a cat.' He whistled. 'But your Orlando, he's not here now?'

She shook her head. 'No.'

'Did he, is he … er …? He isn't dead is he?'

She shook her head. 'He's at school in Durham. He lives there at the school. Then for holidays he goes to his aunt, my husband's sister in Barnard Castle.'

'He got Special Needs? A lad in my class had Special Needs. Couldn't read a letter, couldn't hold a pencil. Had to go off to a living-in school too.'

'No. No. Orlando's very clever. He doesn't have Special Needs.' She peeled the backing off the plaster and covered the cleaned wound. 'Unless his Special Need is to be away from me.'

'Why's that? Why'd he need to be away from you?'

She was silent for a moment. Her glance strayed to the egg but she resisted the impulse to pick it up. 'They said I tried to smother him when he was little. He was nearly dead when they found him. I didn't do it, but there was no

142

telling them. They were very kind, of course. Thomas—my husband—says I was lucky. That anyone else would have ended up behind bars. Even so I was really angry with them all, because they were wrong. I tried to tell them, *him*, the doctors and the police. They didn't like me protesting. *Hysteria*. It's in my notes.'

'That's why they push all the junk into you? To stop you squarking?'

She tore her glance from the egg and turned quickly to stare at the boy. 'Yes, I suppose they do.'

'Tell them no. Keep telling them, Bettina. Dinnet take it. That junk fries your head like an egg.'

'Trying to say no to Thomas is like saying no to a billow of blancmange.'

He laughed at this. 'You're fucken sound, Bettina. I tell you that.' He peered up at her. 'Go on, Bettina. Let us loose and I'll help you clear all this up. Promise.' He smiled. The light streaming through the shattered skylight glinted again on the fine bloom of hair on his cheek.

He was irresistible. She took a deep breath and started to untie him. In minutes he was sitting up on the table rubbing his wrists. Then he jumped down and loomed up before her. For the first time she realised just how tall he was. They stared at each other for a long time. Then he clapped his hands together hard and she jumped. 'Just to get the blood runnin',

143

like,' he grinned. He looked around, shrugged himself out of his parka and draped it over the back of a chair. 'Now then where's your bin, Bettina? You got plastic bags? Dustpan and brush?'

Then together they swept and brushed, bagged and heaved the detritus into the back yard. At the boy's insistence, they tackled the kitchen surfaces and the mountains of dirty dishes and pans. In three hours, a kind of order reigned in the sprawling vicarage kitchen even though cold air was rushing through the hole in the roof.

'Now then,' the boy fished in his pocket and pulled out a battered notebook and scribbled in it with a stubby pencil. He tore off the page and gave it to Bettina. 'Me Uncle Ted. Lives down Hendon. Them low houses, you know? You ring him, Bettina. He'll board up the skylight for now and then rebuild it for you later. You'll have to pay, like. But he's cheap. Cash only, like.'

Bettina hesitated. It was years since she had telephoned anyone except Thomas and her doctor.

He stared at her, nodded, and picked up the phone. 'Here, I'll do it for you.'

She clicked on the kettle and went out to the hall to rummage in an old handbag under the stairs and came back with a leather wallet in her hand. She counted out four twenty -pound notes onto the table. 'For services rendered. Should get you to Edinburgh so you can sell those kites.' she said, smoothing them out in a row. 'I only hope they're still legal tender.'

He was pouring boiling water over bags in a brown tea-pot. 'Why's that?' he said.

'The notes are very old. I was going out to buy myself this new spring coat when that business happened with Orlando, when it all blew up. When they took him away. I've never been out of the house since. Except twice to hospital.'

He handed her a beaker of tea. 'Time you got yourself out and about a bit, Bettina. Remember that adrenaline! Goes fucken bad if you lie around too much. Don't I know it?' He gulped his tea. 'You should teck it steady but mebbe you should go and see him. That Orlando.'

'They won't let me. He ...'

'He'll be dying to see you. I know it.'

'You can't say that.'

He scowled at her. 'I can. Me, I'm dying to see me own mother at this very minute. But I have to go through all those locked doors at Cherry Knowle to do that.'

She knew the hospital. She had been there. Thomas made pastoral visits. 'Well, I ...' her glance wandered away from him and alighted again on the egg in the pink egg-cup.

The boy took her face in his large hands and turned it towards him, away from the egg. 'You should take your time, like I said, Bettina. Give yourself time but just say to yourself you're gunna see that Orlando. For definite.'

When he moved his hands away her cheeks felt very cold. It was years since Thomas had even borne to touch her, flesh on flesh. He was repulsed by her. He quote St Paul. *All flesh is not the same flesh.*

The boy picked up the money and tucked it into the pocket of his parka. 'Ta for this,' he said. He looked round. 'Now then, what about dinner?'

'I don't usually...'

'You sit there, drink your tea and I'll rustle something up.'

For the next twenty minutes he padded round the kitchen as though it were his own. He found two tins of corned beef, some potatoes and dusty carrots and assembled them, decanted and scraped, into a casserole dish. He put the casserole in the top oven of the Aga. 'Fifty minutes', he said. 'I've set your timer.' He stood grinning down at her.

For the first time she started to feel uneasy about the boy. She tucked the stray hair back again under its clip. 'Thomas will be back by then,' she lied. 'Perhaps you'd join us?'

'That's nice but no thanks, Bettina.' He stood up. 'I'd better be off. I got a train to catch. Fucken kites to fly.' He put on his parka and zipped it up. 'I'll call on me uncle down

146

Hendon and tell him about this, then hitch a lift back to Gateshead.'

She took a deep breath, stood, reached across and took the egg from its pink cup. She thrust it into his hand. 'You take this. Treasure it,' she said. 'P'raps you could give it to your mother?'

He looked at the egg, nodded and thrust it into his pocket beside the money. Then she saw him off, waving at him from the door as though he were any routine caller at the vicarage.

It was only as she turned back into the kitchen that she realised the boy had not volunteered his name. She picked up the phone.

'Oh, Bettina!' When Thomas answered the phone his voice was threaded with its usual pleading, gentle panic.

'Thomas?' she said. 'I'm afraid the kitchen ceiling's collapsed... no, no. That won't be necessary. I have arranged for someone to come and make a temporary mend. No ... he's coming round as I speak. He'll mend it properly as soon as possible ... no, no I'm quite all right. Quite ... Thomas? Thomas?'

Me Auntie Milly's house never changes. Like a doll's house is a row of doll's houses. Just one storey high; a door, two windows and a steep roof. Some of the houses in that row have windows cut into the roofs these days, but they look like scars to me. My auntie's house has this flat skylight. My uncle keeps his fish tanks up there.

'Your Uncle Ted's off on a job. That one you rang about ...' Auntie Millie makes an arc, a dragging trail of smoke, in the air with her cigarette as she lets me in. 'Who is this woman...'

'Bettina,' I say. It's a nice name, canny. 'Cash job...'

'Bettina? Funny name that.' She leads me through into her small downstairs room and parks herself in the chair that still has the imprint of her bottom on the battered cushion. She holds out a battered packet of Marlboros and frowns when I turn her offer down. Then she lights a new one herself from the stub of the old one. She takes a deep drag and speaks through the streaming smoke. 'You know this woman, like?'

'You could say that. I do now, anyway.'

'You're a funny'n, you. I always said that. I told our Carol. You've bred a funny'n there. Always cleaning. Sommat not right about that.'

I look round. Aunt Millie's room is neat

148

enough. It smells like our own first house: *potpourri*, burnt gas and cigarette smoke. When I was little I loved to come in to that smell and watch my mother put her cigarette in a saucer to smoulder while she made me my tea. She hugged me a lot in those days and she could really make you laugh.

Then, after that thing happened, Mam took to her couch. She began to see things that weren't there and the room became a war zone around her. Everything dissolved into something different. You could see it in her eyes. My brother and me tried to clean up around her and make her cups of tea to keep her calm. My Dad finally got sick of it all and lit off and only came back when she was sectioned and the police had tracked him down. Then he went off again, down London. That was it for us, my brother and me. The end of the beginning.

Auntie Millie's my mother's younger sister, though you'd think she was older. The last time I saw my mother she was full-faced, smooth skinned and young-looking, even though her glance was vacant and her shuffling way of walking made her seem older. That's down to the drugs, like.

Millie's sharp eyes rake over me. 'What brings you down Sunderland? In bother are yeh, son?'

'No such thing, Auntie. Just down here for a visit.'

'Workin' are yeh?'

'You're jokin'!'

She waves her cigarette, leaving that trail of smoke. 'You should stay on down here, pet. We'd find you a space. Teddy'd find you some work.'

I'm already shaking my head. 'Wouldn't suit, Auntie. Ted can't stand the sight of us.' There have been plenty times down the years when Ted bad-mouthed my Mam or my Dad. My Uncle Ted's your upright, hard-working kind of feller. Collects fish. Need I say more?

'So, you're down to see our Carol?' Millie peers up at me through the smoke that is sitting in the air. 'Gunna visit that place? Gives me the shivers, that place.'

I stare at her, wanting to deny that I'm going to see my mother. Then, out of the blue, I'm back in our old house, on the night it all really started. I've got the kettle on ready to make my Mam a cup of tea when she gets in from the Bingo. We've had two days of snow and the night's dark and freezing, but the gas fire's on, my Dad's safely out at the pub and my brother's at Scouts. I hear the click of the gate as Mam comes in the back yard, then there is this awful racket. Howling. Nine cats have leapt out at her, meowing and howling to get past her through the gate. They've been sheltering in this igloo I've just built between the wash house and the wheelie bin. I've been playing out there all day, building the igloo

150

and making a dry seat from two piles of bricks and a wooden pallet.

Mam's screams pull me pronto out to our narrow yard and there she is, lying in the snow beside my igloo, shuddering and retching. I touch her shoulder but she's already leapt through the night skies onto another planet where I can't reach her.

When I think about it, that was probably the beginning of the end of the beginning. It was after that night that my mother took to her couch. And the rest, as they say, is history.

'So, will you go and see our Carol?' Millie persists here and now. 'In that place?'

My hand, hard inside the pocket of my parka, encounters the egg. 'Aye. I think so.' I turn to go. 'Mebbe I will.'

'Mebbe you'd like a cup of tea?' Millie ventures.

'Nah. I'll get off,' I say.

*   *   *

At the hospital the day room smells of piss, potatoes, Shake'nVac and cheap shampoo. It reminds me of Newcastle Airport in the old days. Artificial flowers, too many seats and not much else. The people wandering through this day room are a bit like travellers themselves. They might not have luggage but sure are in transit from some planet to another. A blonde girl in a green overall who'd be the spit of that

151

girl in Neighbours if it wasn't for the spots, takes me across to my mother, who is sitting with her back to the room, looking out of the window. 'Look, Carol. You've got a visitor.' She looks at me her eyebrows raised.

'She's my mother,' I say.

'Here's your son come to see you, Carol.'

Mam's head turns and she looks at me, smiling slightly. Someone's done her hair up in thick black coils. Her clothes are immaculate. She is wearing powder and pink lipstick. This is a relief. The last time I came she was walking around with her dress tucked in her knickers, all very innocent.

The girl in the green overall is still standing there. 'We're all in our best today, aren't we Carol? The Minister visited us this afternoon. From the Government.'

Mam looks up at her. 'Get away, will you. lass? This is me son. Isn't that what you said? Leave us alone.'

The girl sniffs loudly and stalks away and I sit down on a hard chair by the window. 'Hello Mam,' I say.

She frowns at me. 'Who d'she say you were?'

I look into her dark eyes, my flesh standing out in pimples. Here we go. She frightens me. Every time I see her I feel this fear that makes my hair stand on end.

She's not happy with my silence. 'Why d'you come?' she says sharply. 'Tell us now!'

152

I dip in my pocket and hold out the egg. 'I brought you this egg. It's made of glass.'

She holds it up in a beam of sunlight and the spiral shimmers. She smiles. 'I sold these, you know. Years ago when I worked in Binns. Very popular. They flew off the shelves.' She turns it this way and that, staring at it with her head on one side. I think of Bettina with the egg in her mouth. 'Thank you, son.' Mam looks me straight in the eye. Her eyes are bright. 'What's that plaster? Have you hurt yourself? Shouldn't you be at school? I have two sons, you know. Two sons of my own. They go to school. The youngest, he likes building snow houses. Loves it, snow.'

I stand up quickly and the chair scrapes and tips up behind me. 'I have to go, Mam.'

'You're going. Why are you going?' Her voice becomes young, high-toned like a bird.

'I have to go and fly some kites.' I start to walk quickly down the long room.

Her voice travels after me. 'Kites? Kites? Lovely, that. Kites!'

At the door I turn round again but she is concentrating on the egg, turning it this way and that in the light from the window.

I am nearly at the hospital gates when the girl in the green overall catches up with me. She thrusts the egg into my hand. 'Your mother can't have this,' she says. 'Are you stupid or what?'

'Why not?' I say. 'It's a gift.'

153

'It's glass,' she says. 'Glass is not allowed. You won't believe what they get up to, with glass. It's very dangerous. You should think on.' She pauses. 'We had to rive it off her, you know. She got quite excited about that egg. They had to sedate her.'

'Right,' I say. I pushed it deep into the pocket of my parka, keeping it tight in my hand. 'I suppose you're right.'

Then, with her still standing there, I turn and set off again for the dual carriageway, thumb at the ready.

12 Jetsam

The second time the American comes to my house, I have abandoned my romantic fantasy—born on a weird six hour train journey from Wales—of a high brow intellectual affair, and embarked on more down-to-earth friendships. You can only take so much intellectual intensity with no physical reward.

When I first met him on the train I had just slipped off my boots when I noticed him, sitting opposite me. Even sitting down you could tell he was tall and gangly. He had rimless glasses and a whispy blond beard. I tipped my books onto the table. *Jane Austen. Sylvia Plath. Joseph Heller.*

'Oh, *really*?' The voice was American, a soft West Coast sound. 'You people really *read* these things?' He leaned across and picked up the Sylvia Plath. The fingers were implausibly long and tapered.

I was flattered by his response. I had magazines at the bottom of my cotton sack but my instinct had been to show off my good taste to this promising audience. I was very young then.

He said something about Sylvia Plath being a control freak but a genius and we went on to talk the whole journey. To be honest, he did nine tenths of the talking. His soft voice washed over me as he held forth about English and American literature and the need for excellence and purity in all things. He told me he loved scholarship but had abandoned college early because of the invasive presence of other boys, beefy and tiresome. And he told me how he had to pull his curtains against the Californian light so he could write. Writing was his vocation. He did not publish because he thought that was a betrayal of his art. He worked in an art gallery which gave him time to write.

I was entranced.

My mother, on time as always, picked me up off the train. After telling her my Welsh grandmother was in good form, I told her about the American. 'He's on his way to Scotland. Been to Lyme Regis, then Wales. Just wandering about all summer. How cool is that?'

'How old is he?'

An unusual question. My mother's usually more laid back than that. We've been on our own forever and she's the best mate a daughter could have, and never po-faced.

'He's really old. Twenty-five, thirty, maybe.' I took a sheet out of my bag. 'He wrote down this list of what I should read.' I pushed it under her nose. The page of his writing was like a delicate work of art.

'I said he would call here on his way back,' I

added.

She raised her eyebrows.

'He's really something,' I said. 'You'll see.'

'Well, if he does come, you can take care of him yourself.'

On the first morning of his visit my mother sent me to his room with his breakfast on a tray but he insisted in coming into the kitchen and eating at the table.

I was tucking into my breakfast and she was leaning against the sink. I thought how pretty she was despite being so old. 'Nice morning?' she said, smiling at him.

He looked at her over rimless glasses and nodded. 'So it is,' he drawled.

I dipped my head over my porridge.

The American stayed three nights. My mother managed to squeeze a few words out of him about the importance of us getting out of Iraq but apart from that he spent time with me in the dining room, mentoring me about critical points of English and American literature before he went off upstairs to his bedroom, closed the curtains and wrote into the night.

Being with him was heavy-going but enjoyable, like a walk on the top of the moors. I thought my head would burst with all these sparkling ideas and took no notice of my mother's concerned looks. I was in love.

Even after he had departed his unique coaching during the summer secured me good exam results so I could apply to a better university. Then throughout the next year letters arrived in his tiny handwriting: scraps of prose; allusions to books and the idiocy of writers.

I forced my mother to read them. 'Well?'

'He's very clever, quirky.' she said slowly. 'Original. Maybe he's crazy.'

Then in my first year at my very good university I continued to concoct my own pretentious, prosy responses to his letters. These were very different from the newsy letters I wrote to my mother, who was missing me desperately. She wrote: *I take pleasure in you being there, love, but I'm enduring this low tide feeling. I miss my little comrade, my fellow conspirator, my partner in pleasure'*.

But in my second term, as I passed my first exams and had my first, then my second, passionate affair, my replies to the American stopped and my letters to my mother slowed down. Life for me was very exciting.

And here we are on my first long vacation and the American has turned up again. He has to have my room because the spare room is occupied by two boys from college who are visiting and want to do a bit of climbing on the fells. I jump into bed with my mother and we talk till the early hours about all that changes in our lives and all that remains the same.

The American seems old and strange, blinking at me through his rim-less glasses.

I rage with my mother about him turning up without warning and then I go off with my mates for two days walking and climbing. When we come back, exhilarated and muddy, the American and my mother are in the dining room, talking. When I open the door they look up at me as though I am a Martian. My mother's cheeks are pink and her eyes are bright.

Later, when she comes to join me in our shared bedroom she is still smiling. 'That is an interesting man, you know,' she says. She has a paper in her hand. 'Look! He's given me a reading list. He's off in the morning but he says he'll certainly write.'